ALSO BY JOYCE CAROL OATES

Novels

With Shuddering Fall (1964)
A Garden of Earthly Delights (1967)
Expensive People (1968)
Them (1969)
Wonderland (1971)
Do With Me What You Will (1973)
The Assassins (1975)
Childwold (1976)
The Triumph of the Spider Monkey (1976)
Son of the Morning (1978)

Stories

By the North Gate (1963)
Upon the Sweeping Flood (1966)
The Wheel of Love (1970)
Marriages and Infidelities (1972)
The Hungry Ghosts (1974)
The Goddess and Other Women (1974)
The Seduction and Other Stories (1975)
The Poisoned Kiss (1975)
Crossing the Border (1976)
Night-Side (1977)
All the Good People I've Left Behind (1979)

Poetry

Women in Love (1968)
Anonymous Sins (1969)
Love and Its Derangements (1970)
Angel Fire (1973)
Dreaming America (1973)
The Fabulous Beasts (1975)
Season of Peril (1977)
Women Whose Lives are Food,
    Men Whose Lives are Money (1978)

Criticism

The Edge of Impossibility (1972)
The Hostile Sun: The Poetry of D.H. Lawrence (1973)
New Heaven, New Earth (1974)

Drama

Miracle Play (1974)

Editor

Scenes From American Life (1973)
The Best American Short Stories (1979)

Joyce Carol Oates

CYBELE

Santa Barbara

BLACK SPARROW PRESS

1979

ACKNOWLEDGEMENT

"The Key" originally appeared in *Weekend Magazine* (July 1978) and in *Punch* (January 1979) under the title "Conquistador."

LIBRARY OF CONGRESS CATALOGING IN PUBLICATION DATA

Oates, Joyce Carol, 1938-
  Cybele.

  I. Title.
PZ4.O122Cy [PS3565.A8]   813'.5'4   79-20305
ISBN 0-87685-424-2 (paper)
ISBN 0-87685-425-0 (trade cloth)
ISBN 0-87685-426-9 (signed cloth)

for the Edwins—

TABLE OF CONTENTS

Cybele

I.

In Memoriam: Edwin Locke

There was a lover of mine who worshipped me, and became reckless with his life, which was soon taken from him—more abruptly than I would have wished, and more cruelly; for I came to pity him in the end.

It was said by many people that his premature death was a tragic one. It was frightful, and pointless, and certainly very ugly. A disgraceful end, some said. And how especially horrible for his children, and his former wife. . . . No one seems to have said it was an appropriate death though we know that all deaths are appropriate.

His business associates were incredulous, and saddened, like his former neighbors; his children were stricken with grief and will not readily cast off their father's shame; his wife was—if not surprised, shocked. Most bitter of all deaths are those that cannot be mourned, and cannot even be spoken of.

There are tears of grief that are tears of fury as well. But they are not cleansing. Nor does the earth greedily soak them up.

Perhaps there were those who mocked his death . . . ?

And we know there were those who profited by it.

Edwin Locke. It is a technique, I understand, to describe individuals as they make their appearance in a narrative. But Edwin hovers in my mind's eye apart from his story—which is a complicated one and which, accelerating as it does, will leave him somewhat out of breath, and his features indistinct; near the end no one will *see* him at all and he certainly will have lost even his incomplete vision of himself. (My difficulty is that I see him so clearly, so vividly. He exists, still, he has not really died, so long as I can summon him back. I must resist the temptation to assume that you can see him as I do . . . and that you can know him as I knew him.)

And yet—how can I describe him?

He looked like so many men.

Though he thought of himself as unique, and had a habit of glancing into mirrors from the side as if hoping to confirm his uniqueness—was it a jaunty quirky arrangement of features, was it an unconscious scowl, or an especially "intelligent" look about the eyes—he looked like so many men, I am amused and baffled by him: what did *he* see, or imagine he saw, when he studied his reflection? A large mild hopeful face, blunt-boned. A coarse but not unattractive complexion. Dark hair, graying unevenly, wavy and still thick—which pleased his vanity, of course. His eyes were the color of the sea: blue-gray, gray-blue, neutral at times as a sunless sky. (He thought of them as blue, and listed *blue* on his driver's license and passport.) There were creases on his forehead that first appeared when he was in his early twenties, studying economics at Harvard, but, curiously enough, these creases did not deepen appreciably in the years that followed. So he looked, until the last months of his life, engagingly young; even, when he smiled (and he smiled frequently), boyish. His mouth was fairly strong in repose but vulnerable at other times. When he laughed, unaware, his teeth were bared like a skull's—big broad white heedless teeth. His nose was perhaps his least attractive feature, being somewhat large, and coarse-pored; and the nostrils appeared to be, at times, unnaturally wide and dark. (Edwin had an unconscious habit of breathing deeply and sharply through his nose, causing the nostrils to flare, when he was thinking stern thoughts. And at such times the creases in his forehead deepened alarmingly.)

12

At his heaviest he weighed 185 pounds. His shoulders were wide, but somewhat sloping. Across his back freckles and moles had been scattered, like paint drops flicked from a brush, carelessly, rather charmingly. He believed himself tall though in fact he was only slightly more than six feet. He *liked* himself—by no means a universal human condition. (At least he liked to say that he liked himself.) Since boyhood he had whispered to himself, and gesticulated, in bathroom mirrors: so he "rehearsed" the day before him. Sometimes his stare was searching and suspicious, at other times it dissolved in a fond forgiving grin. He *did* like himself. He *was* a handsome man, and his life had turned out well—an excellent marriage, two marvelous sons, a successful career with another promotion probably within the next two years. And of course he dressed well. He did not fuss about clothes but his wife Cynthia took pride in outfitting him with nearly as much fastidious concern as she outfitted herself. His favorite suit was made of the softest imaginable wool, a very dark blue, tailored for him in Bond Street, London, during a holiday he and Cynthia took at the time of her fortieth birthday.

He played handball. And squash. And for a while in his mid-thirties forced himself to rise early, at dawn, and go swimming at a YMCA near his office—but within a few months he lost interest in the sessions, which had for him the queer diffused hallucinatory nature of a dream gone wrong. Half-naked, in fact nearly naked, in a pool of bright riotous water that stank, and stung the eyes, splashing about, groping about, in the company of other nearly naked men, gasping for air, panting, unable to stop himself from imagining a fish-slender adolescent self swimming effortlessly before him, all mocking elbows and toes—no, the sessions wearied him, and alarmed him, since they caused him to feel his age. Sometimes he played golf, but he could not help thinking that it was a waste of time. And the handball and squash—well, that

13

was a waste of time too. He enjoyed shooting a few baskets with Teddie and Donald, sometimes, on Saturday morning, over at the junior high playground. The boys were pleased to be seen with their father, and it pleased Edwin that he could teach them something. (Donald, the elder son was a promising basketball player, in his father's opinion.) For a brief while Edwin and Cynthia had gone cross-country skiiing with two other couples, but when Edwin fell on a particularly rocky slope in the Pine Hollow sanctuary, and badly sprained his ankle—the poor man had a vision, an instantaneous vision, of raw white bone piercing his flesh, and had screamed aloud at the horror of it—he lost all enthusiasm for the sport, and never regained it. Such activities were, after all, a waste of time, and hadn't he begun to notice that time seemed to be passing more and more quickly....

He began working for Monarch Life & Auto Insurance in 1964, and moved with them to their new building in Wainboro, a suburb some nineteen miles from the rather more fashionable suburb, Woodland, where he and his family lived. Though it has become almost obligatory for men in Edwin's position to speak in a deprecatory way of their work, and to half-apologize for their affluence, the truth was that Edwin liked what he did: he considered himself, not without a small surge of vanity, as a man who *liked* his life and nearly every aspect of it. He did not whine, he did not indulge in "self-pity," it could never have been pointed out to him that his employment on a high managerial level at Monarch Life was in any way a waste of his time, or of his spirit—he took pride, in fact, in being so well-adjusted, so normal, in an era in which (as he read in popular magazines, and on the feature and editorial pages of newspapers) "long-established values were being questioned." For many years, peaking in his mid-thirties, he had been extremely interested in, perhaps even obsessed by, the stock market—in imitation of his father,

14

perhaps, who had done so extraordinarily well though he had had, at the start, only a modest amount of capital to invest. Edwin had done less well, but the adventure of it excited him, at least for a while, until a half-year of recession discouraged him from further investments; and though he always denied it, Cynthia was perfectly right when she attributed his stomach disorders (for an unnerving period Edwin was certain he was developing ulcers) to the capricious market of those dark months. At the time of his death Edwin's personal savings and assets had considerably diminished, of course, but at his wealthiest—at the age of forty-four, before he conceived of, and consummated, his passion for me—he was worth approximately three-quarters of a million dollars.

He was to die suddenly at the age of forty-six. Recalling him, her voice tremulous, her expression grave, Gladys, one of the older secretaries at Monarch Life, was to speak of how often he remained late at work, well past seven; and once (she had left the office at five, had gone shopping in the underground mall near the Monarch Building, and returned to her car in the employees' parking lot much later) she had seen him walking to the executives' corner of the lot with his head bowed and a queer bemused smile stretching his lips. It was nearly dark, the day had been chill and blustery, but Edwin Locke walked with his topcoat unbuttoned and his tie blowing back over his shoulder; his gaze, fastened to the oil-stained pavement, was curiously intent, even quizzical, as if he were searching, there, in the pavement, for something no one else might see. Maybe he had, already, a premonition of his death, the woman said softly. They say—I read somewhere—your death casts a kind of shadow back over you—I mean from the future— So maybe poor Mr. Locke—

But no. Not at all. At that very moment he was thinking of me.

15

II.

The Tower

The tower: thirty storeys high. From this distance it appears to gleam with hidden sunlight, lifting above the small, diminished buildings that surround it. Holding a folded newspaper to shield his face from the rain Edwin Locke stares and wonders, is it possible—is it possible that Cathleen is looking out the hotel window at this moment—or was the room facing another side? In his agitation he can't quite remember. Room 1631. He *did* see a jetliner passing very near the window on Monday, when he secured the room, but the room might have been facing the other end of the airport; and the airport is, of course, enormous, a veritable city. He has been so accustomed to travelling by air that the routine, the drive out from Wainboro in the company limousine, the wait for his flight, the flight itself, have ceased to make much of an impression on him: he continues to work, of course, and only about midway in the flight does he allow himself the pleasure of a martini and the *New York Times*, which he will read very nearly in its entirety, though he never has any time for attending galleries or plays or films on his business trips. As the years have passed, however, the airport has evidently grown; he would perhaps not have started out on foot for the airport hotel if he'd known how difficult it was going to be to get to it. Especially in this sudden cold rain, extraordinarily cold for mid-October. Especially since there does not appear to be any direct route by which one can get to the hotel on foot.

17

A tower of onyx and jade and glass, and poured concrete. Rising effortlessly above the smaller hangars and service buildings connected with the airport. A striking building, its windows vertical slashes that, oddly, appear to be both darkened and yet filled with light, a blackly-glowing light, possibly an accident of clouds and sun—it is early afternoon but because of the sudden rain the sky has turned opaque, and the feel of the day is of dusk; yet the sun has managed to pierce some of the clouds and random, faint fingers of intense light are moving across the landscape. Edwin shivers, squinting at the tower. It isn't very likely that Cathleen would be looking out the window; if she were, she would probably be watching the sky, watching the enormous silver planes taking off and landing. And there is the possibility—of which he doesn't want to think—that she has given up on him and gone home.

He hurries. Has been hurrying. Newspaper in one hand, briefcase in the other. Along this stretch there are no sidewalks, only a very muddy road, and every few seconds— literally *seconds*—a cab or a van or a private car honks irritably for him to get to the side, and he steps reluctantly onto the curb. He must avoid both the filthy gutter and the muddy, debris-strewn ground; and there is the danger of being splashed by drivers who are certainly violating the 20-mile-an-hour speed zone. His left trouser leg is uncomfortably wet already—a squad car sped by, and sheets of dirty water from puddles lifted on either side like transparent wings.

In New York City he considered placing a call to Cathleen, at home; it was only 11 A.M. then and she wouldn't have left for the hotel. But the prospect somehow unnerved him: he wanted her so badly, he loved her so much, it had taken hours of persuasion to get her to agree to his plan—that he return on Thursday, instead of Friday (when his wife expected him back)—he could not possibly risk her changing her mind. "But if someone sees us," she said. "No one will see us: we'll stay

18

in the room all day. We won't leave the room at all," Edwin said, squeezing her cold hands in his, smiling anxiously, trying to get her to look at him, to look him in the eye: then he would wink, and they would both dissolve in laughter. He loved her so much, he was fairly trembling with emotion, and with desire; yet he would not force her, he would not bully her, as she indicated, elliptically, other men had done from time to time, including her husband. "We won't have to leave the room," Edwin whispered, kissing her fingers. Dizziness rose like a vapor; he felt suddenly short of breath; he hugged Cathleen and buried his face against her wavy pale hair, and took strength from her: her unresisting warmth, her very being. "I love you so much," he said. "I just can't . . . . I can't explain. . . ." Her hair smelled absolutely clean: it smelled like nothing at all.

Then, as if deeply moved by his passion, Cathleen had slipped her arms around him and held him close to her, close to her. And so she acquiesced. She too trembled: faintly she whispered *I love you.*

The flight which was to leave Kennedy Airport at 11:30 was delayed, though Edwin had been assured that morning it would leave exactly on time. *Then* he should have telephoned Cathleen, simply to explain that he'd be late; but he wasn't sure if she would be at home, or on her way to the airport (which was a considerable distance from Woodland). Still, he might have left a message for her at the hotel desk. . . . But he didn't want one of the desk clerks to take down the message, it would be so embarrassingly obvious that "Albert Wain" was arranging for an assignation in room 1631, and that he was inexperienced at such things, inept and perhaps a bit amusing. He should have devised some sort of code with Cathleen so that they could communicate without fear of detection. . . .

The plane had left New York after a delay of only twenty

19

minutes; but it had been forced to circle this airport for a half-hour; so, as soon as he disembarked (Edwin was one of the first of the passengers to leave, he had in fact been rather peremptory in getting ahead of others, which was not characteristic of him) he telephoned the hotel from the terminal. Room 1631, please. Would the switchboard operator ring that room, please.... So he waited, standing with the receiver pressed to his ear, staring at an illuminated, revolving advertisement for a new brand of cigarettes, and as the phone rang at the other end, a small sad inadequate sound, he felt his heartbeat accelerating at an almost alarming pace. She was not there. She had left, angry with him for being late. Or, what was worse: she had never come at all. This very morning, perhaps, she had woken to the realization that she did not love him, she did not love him well enough to risk her marriage.... Sweating, Edwin turned away from the cigarette advertisement, which was dancing and flashing in his eyes. He saw, in the crowded waiting room, making his way toward him, a Woodland neighbor... not a friend but an acquaintance, whose wife Cynthia halfway liked, or at any rate sometimes invited to bridge luncheons at their house, though rarely to evening parties: she simply did not like the husband that well, and Edwin had no opinion one way or the other. A man like himself, more or less, a few years older, part-owner of a fairly successful real estate agency in Woodland. He had not noticed Edwin, who turned discreetly away. ...And what if he had seen him, Edwin reasoned, what difference would it make, surely there was nothing extraordinary about his making a telephone call; and it wasn't likely that his being back home a day earlier would be remarked upon.

No answer in room 3016, the operator told him.

But he had wanted room 1630, Edwin said. Had she been ringing the wrong room?

1630?

20

No—it was 1631. It was 1631 he wanted.

So the operator rang this number and it was busy. Edwin's eyelids fluttered with an emotion he could not comprehend—it might have been exasperation, it might have been violent relief. Cathleen was in the room, then. Waiting for him. She hadn't gone home, she hadn't changed her mind.... Unless of course someone else was in the room. But would they have put another party in that room when Edwin had specifically asked for it, had reserved it on Monday, when "Albert Wain" had even paid for it in advance, in cash... when the girl at the desk had assured him....

Should she keep ringing, the operator asked, or would he like to place another call in a few minutes?

Keep ringing.

She *must* be there. He tried to picture her: a tall, fair-skinned woman in her thirties, her brown-blond hair cut fashionably short about her delicate face, her expression grave... or playful... or loving.... One of the last times they had met, in Woodland's most costly grocer's, between aisles of imported jams and jellies and tinned biscuits, he had caught sight of her at the very moment she saw him, and his heart leapt at her beauty: she *was* a beautiful woman, he had not imagined it, he had not dreamt and plotted and tortured himself for weeks in pursuit of a woman not worthy of his passion. Her face appeared to brighten, her very gaze seemed to catch fire, at least for a moment. Then she began to blush. And rather gravely smiled. And after they exchanged nervous, stammering greetings, she called to her daughter Crystal—a child of four, tall for her age, and very pretty—to come over and meet Mr. Locke.

Afterward, when he talked her into allowing him to buy ice cream for the girl, and coffee for both of them, she responded to Edwin's half-teasing remark that he was delighted to have come upon the two of them, accidentally, did Crystal usually

21

accompany her mother to the grocery store?—with a teasing smile of her own.

Sometimes, she said.

Then he was particularly lucky today, wasn't he.

The little girl's hair was bouncy, and very blond: several shades lighter than her mother's. She appeared not to be shy of Edwin in the slightest, and queried him as she ate her strawberry sundae about his children, and where he lived, and did they have a dog. Bold but sweet. *Very* pretty. Edwin tried to disguise his irritation, that Cathleen had brought the girl along and more or less forced him to speak circumlocutiously; he tried to hide his eagerness to get her to leave the table and investigate a counter of stuffed animals—would she like to pick out one, maybe one of the smaller ones? (There were pandas four feet high, and gaudy drunken-eyed rabbits with pink fur, the size of beagles.) Only then could he manage to squeeze Cathleen's hand under the table.

That day, she had not exactly agreed to his plan. She had blushed, and stammered that she didn't know—she didn't know—it was true that she thought of him constantly now, and it was true that she no longer loved her husband, but at the same time— There was so much risk involved, there was so much danger—

"But I love you," Edwin said quietly. "You must know that. I want to marry you. These past few weeks I've been able to keep going only by telling myself that it isn't impossible, our getting married. You *must* know—"

She started to speak but went silent. She stared at the glass top of the little wrought-iron table, and allowed him to speak earnestly to her, in a quick desperate undertone, until Crystal ran back hugging a stuffed giraffe with a fringe for a mane and a price-tag of $35.

As he had hoped, the fact that he wanted to marry her before they were even lovers in a technical sense, while it alarmed

22

her at first, eventually impressed her, and assured her that his love was absolutely genuine.

So she agreed, finally, to meet him at the hotel. The newest one, the black-and-green-and-glass tower. She *did* feel a great deal for him—she loved him, perhaps. And so of course she must be in the room as they had planned. (And how complicated the plan became for Edwin—far more complicated than it needed to be. He had had to tell all sorts of unanticipated lies to secretaries and associates at both ends, and lived in dread of hearing, when he went to the office on Friday afternoon, that the New York office had tried to reach him Thursday afternoon. Or that, for some inexplicable reason, Cynthia had tried to reach him in New York City on Thursday afternoon or Friday morning. . . .)

The telephone in room 1631 was still busy. Finally Edwin hung up, and grabbed his briefcase, and hurried out. He was so agitated that he could not even wait for a taxi—all the available taxis were taken, and there was a considerable queue at the curb; the limousine for downtown was no use to him; and of course the company limousine wasn't there. So he would walk. He could get to the hotel much more quickly by walking, even in the rain. And such was his anxiety, and the feeling of constriction in his chest and throat, that he believed the exercise would do him a great deal of good.

I love you so much, he whispered.

□ □ □

He hurries. Has been hurrying. Now he is confronted by a sort of cloverleaf or round-about—not so intimidating as the multi-levelled circles out at the interstate expressway (where once even his chauffeur made an error, exiting at the right exit for the airport but unaccountably drifting into the northbound

23

lane of the exit, so that he wound up driving miles out of his way, and Edwin was nearly late for his flight) but intimidating nevertheless. Hard to believe, Edwin thinks, that so many people are going to the airport at this particular time of day; and it's only a Thursday; surely weekend traffic hasn't begun. Going to the airport or leaving the airport. Steady streams of traffic: cabs, private cars, trucks, buses, even motorcycles. Some drive with their headlights on; the sky has been steadily darkening.

He stands, poised, ready to sprint across the lanes of pavement. The hotel is fairly close now, he should have no difficulty once he crosses the street, surely traffic will let up in another minute. . . . He forces himself to be patient. She *is* in the room; perhaps she has ordered drinks for them both, from room service. It occurred to him shortly after hanging up the phone that she was probably on the line inquiring about the flight—she would know, then, that it had been delayed, she would know that passengers had just disembarked. Though she would not know that he'd be coming on foot, and would be rather wet, she might very likely assume that he would like a drink; in his place, her own husband, surely, would prefer a martini. . . .

Jet-liners overhead. One from the north, followed almost at once by one from the east. Edwin's teeth rattle though he is only half-conscious of the noise. If only the traffic would let up . . . perhaps after this Greyhound bus. . . . He steps out onto the pavement, rather timorously. But a truck bearing down upon him forces him back almost at once. And splashes his legs.

Bastard.

Then he notices an underpass—some thirty yards to the right.

But he discovers, when he hurries to it, that it is only the beginning of an underpass. Steps leading down to a tunnel, but a sawhorse forbidding entry. Rusted girders. Flapping plastic sheets. Evidently this area isn't completed. . . . Across the busy cloverleaf, adjacent to the hotel, there will be an enormous multi-levelled car park; construction is fairly well along on the car park, but seems to have been halted over here. In fact the ground on this side, though bulldozed and levelled long ago, has been allowed to go wild again: field grass and weeds grow freely, there are thistles that have reached a height of six feet or more. Debris is everywhere: newspapers and boxes and Styrofoam containers, and even what looks like part of an outdoor barbecue, and what surely *is* part of a baby buggy. Garbage. Discarded spikes, turned to rust. Pieces of glass.

And it is muddy. Very muddy. Edwin steps unwisely backward and his feet sink, and when he pulls them out they make ugly sucking sounds.

Why the hell isn't that underpass in operation, he thinks. It would be so easy, so absurdly easy, to get to the hotel if only the underpass . . . if only. . . . He grimaces, staring at the hotel. From this angle it looks hardly closer than it had looked five minutes ago. Above it, suddenly, a massive jet-liner appears, and for a terrible instant Edwin thinks it is going to crash into the building. He flinches and cries aloud, like a child. But of course the liner will clear the building easily, of course there is no danger. It appears to float. It veers down past the hotel, deceptively silent, its silver wings gleaming boldly and rather beautifully, as Edwin stares. An object in a dream, weightless, with an eerie indefinable grace. He wonders, in the instant before its incredible roar obliterates all thought, whether Cathleen is watching it land, and whether its size and nearness frightened her. . . . If they were in the room together he would reach out instinctively to grasp her hand.

The danger of their meeting in public, or at the homes of mutual friends: that he might, instinctively, without being

25

able to stop himself, take her hand. Or touch her arm, or her shoulder. Or lean forward to kiss her. In the several months of his love for her he had noticed himself bringing her name up, often at inappropriate times; had Cynthia been more perceptive, or had she been jealous of him, she would certainly have guessed what the situation was. But his infatuation for Cathleen had the effect of making him, in general, more emotional—soft-spoken, courteous, sadly observant of his wife, his wife as a woman whom he no longer loved; he found himself in a way more loving to her, as one might be loving, or affectionate, with a sick child or animal whose ignorance of his own condition makes it all the more poignant. And he *did* love Cynthia, still. . . . There was a part of him that would always love her.

They had been married fifteen years, after all. And had known each other for a considerable period of time before. Perhaps that was the trouble, Edwin came to think, as time passed, he and Cynthia had been friends before their marriage, they had drifted into "love" rather than fallen into it, their union was altogether too reasonable, too sane. Both families had been delighted. Cynthia's father, a tax lawyer who made a very good income indeed (among his clients were the state's most famous philanthropist, and the chairman of the board of one of the area's most successful corporations), was especially pleased: he thought of Edwin as a son, the kind of son he had hoped for. (His own son, Cynthia's younger brother, had become an Anglican priest but dropped out of the priesthood and was living now somewhere in Ceylon.) Edwin's mother was sincerely fond of Cynthia, and of course the grandchildren delighted her. Edwin had always been proud of his wife: her intelligence, her warm, pleasing personality, her sense of humor, her appearance. While not a beautiful woman she was certainly very attractive, and during the early years of their marriage he had been, from time to time, rather jealous of the

26

attention men paid her, particularly the somewhat older husbands in their circle of friends. He had even confronted her, once, with a stammering accusation of . . . . But of course he had half-known that it was preposterous, and . . . and in any case . . . in any case the scene that followed pleased them both, in very different ways. For years afterward it became one of their pet allusions, Edwin's "jealousy," and Cynthia's supposed attractiveness to other men.

Of course he was drawn to women, occasionally. Over the years. As what man is not, no matter how contentedly married . . . ? Office-workers, waitresses, the wives of his business associates and friends; beautiful women encountered at large, gay parties, the wives of men he didn't know, would never meet. He was an attractive man, after all, and he knew how to talk to women, how to make simple silly jokes, how to put people at their ease, downplaying himself and his accomplishments, smiling easily, and deeply; though he was not always interested in the people he met, he made an effort to draw them out, and he gave every appearance of listening with genuine interest. It was said of Edwin Locke that he was a charming man; Cynthia's friends spoke of him to her as one of the nicer husbands. (There were nice husbands, and not-so-nice husbands.) "They say I'm very fortunate to have you," Cynthia said wryly.

Though other women attracted him, at times rather strongly, Edwin had never pursued any of them; he had never even contemplated an affair. And then suddenly he had fallen in love with Cathleen Diehl. Charles Diehl's wife. He woke one day to realize he was in love, that it had *happened.* To him. Not only did he dream of the woman, but he found himself planning and plotting and calculating: when would they meet again, who was giving a party this weekend, was it too soon to suggest to Cynthia that they invite the Diehls over. . . . He met her at the golf club one June afternoon, and she struck him as surpassingly lovely: in a denim skirt, a plain but probably quite costly blue jersey blouse, with a necklace of knobby beads or shells around her slender neck. He hadn't known quite what to say. The usual questions: how was her husband, her family, what plans had they for the summer.... The necklace intrigued him. Or he behaved as if it did. Was it Mexican? It was most unusual, most.... She told him, blushing, that it was from Peru. Charles had bought it on one of his trips. It was made not of beads but of carved nuts, nuts hard as stone, if one looked closely enough tiny faces could be seen ... dim, vague, dream-like suggestions of half-human faces....

Very beautiful, Edwin murmured, not knowing what he said.

It might have been that day. Or at an outdoor party the following weekend, where he found himself watching her for long minutes at a time, as she talked with Cynthia, smiling more easily than she did in his presence: yet still with that faint surprised blush to her cheeks which made her look so young. (Though she was nearly, he believed, his own wife's age.) Porcelain-smooth skin, dark intelligent eyes, a melodic voice; and she had a habit, which he came to love, of not exactly completing her sentences but allowing them to trail off, as if she somehow expected her words to suggest themselves, even to present themselves, spontaneously in her listeners' minds. Cynthia found the habit annoying but Edwin defended her, cautiously: Maybe she's just shy, she's always struck me as rather reserved.... No, it's just laziness, Cynthia said curtly. Laziness and arrogance.

And there was the Saturday morning at the Village Pharmacy when a slender teenaged girl in jeans and a striped cotton blouse, her amber-tinted sunglasses charmingly atop her head, turned from the cashier to face Edwin and become—incredibly, wonderfully—Cathleen Diehl. Edwin's pleased astonishment must have shown in his face. He could hardly speak, and then words tumbled from him. How was she, how

28

was Charles, where was she going now, would she mind if he walked along with her. . . .

Then he telephoned her. And made nervous jokes. And asked if they might meet: for lunch, or a drink. Or just to talk. Though she refused him she did not seem very surprised; nor was she surprised when he called again, and still again. Might they meet in some public place, for instance the Village library . . . or in the little square across the street from the library. . . . There was Weber's Cheese House, and the Village Music Shoppe; the cocktail lounge of the Ethan Allen Inn; the children's playground on the banks of the little stream that flowed through Woodland's main park. Might they meet? For just a few minutes? He had something he must tell her, something he could no longer keep to himself.

So he fell in love. It happened. And he realized that it had never *happened* before to him—it was an entirely new, an entirely unanticipated experience. He wanted only to be with her constantly, to talk with her, to hold her. Of course (he would not have denied it) he felt a very strong sexual attraction for her, and in fact dreamt and brooded over her body more or less constantly; but it was not primarily sexual experience he wanted. He wanted instead—he wanted—what?—to be her husband; to be married to her. He wanted her. It was clear, it was inevitable, he wanted *her*, and no other woman.

"But we don't know each other that well," she said slowly.

"Of course we know each other," Edwin said, gripping her arm.

He laughed an abrupt jagged helpless laugh. His eyes were bloodshot from sleeplessness, from lust.

Am I a clown, at the age of forty-four, he wondered. Gazing at his reflection in the mirror he could not really pity himself: his love for Cathleen was too certain, too steadying. Beside it, nothing else mattered greatly. His work, his love for Cynthia, his love for his boys. . . . A clown, a lover. A well-intentioned

29

fool. He studied his face, turning it from side to side. He had not changed. But he *had* changed. His pale blue eyes were quick with hope, moist with absurd plans. It was not too late in his life, surely. He was still a relatively young man, and the boys would understand if he explained it to them carefully enough (hadn't many of their classmates' parents gotten divorces, hadn't it become an altogether accepted thing), and perhaps even Cynthia . . . perhaps, if he explained it all carefully enough, even Cynthia would understand.

I've fallen in love for the first time in my life. There is nothing more to say.

There is nothing more to say. . . .

He is about to dash across the road, braving the traffic and puddles and the stink of exhaust, when a workman in a van drives up, and stops. Where is he headed?—would he like a ride? Edwin groans with relief and gratitude and climbs in, and the workman—small, almost elfin, in greasy coveralls and a denim cap pulled low over his low forehead—tells him to be certain to shut the door hard, so that the lock clicks; and almost before Edwin can thrust the newspaper into his briefcase to get it out of his hands, and adjust his damp rumpled clothing, and wipe his face, and smooth his disheveled hair back from his forehead—almost before he is able to remark upon the van's inspired hairpin-turn maneuvers on the cloverleaf, the little man is saying with a pleased smile: "Here you are, sir. Your destination, sir."

The rain has stopped. The sky, not yet clear, is nevertheless glowing with a pale, stern light.

Edwin thanks the man profusely, and tries to press a bill into his hand. But the man pushes it away almost irritably. "No *thank* you, sir. That isn't called for."

The tower at last. Even at its base it is prodigiously attractive: landscaped with uniformly sculptured evergreens, and ornamental squares and rectangles of bright green grass, perfect as the top of a billiard table; brightened with a fountain upon which, even in daylight, pastel-colored lights play; given a somewhat exotic, perhaps Moorish touch by walls of mosaic tile in onyx and jade and gold. Edwin alights from the mud-splattered van humbly. He hopes no one will notice his arrival. How awkward, that the workman, meaning only to be kind, has let him out at the very center of the hotel's complex system of revolving doors. . . .

On either side are limousines, and handsome private cars, and cabs from which well-dressed men and women are climbing; helping them with their luggage, and pushing coat-racks on wheels, are liveried doormen and busboys, all black, all wide-shoulders and tall and briskly efficient. The head doorman himself, in an outfit trimmed with gold braid, and a dove-grey cap with a smart black visor, smiles at Edwin and asks him for his bag; but Edwin pretends not to hear. Half-crouching he hurries into the hotel.

And now to room 1631. And now to Cathleen.

The hotel is as impressive inside as out: it boasts a thirteen-storey atrium, miniature orange trees, a waterfall, more Moorish tile, Shasta daisies in earthenware pots, macaws of extraordinary colors—bright red, yellow, blue, green—in lacy wicker cages that hang suspended in air. On Monday, when Edwin acquired the room, a convention of neurosurgeons had taken over most of the lobby, and the Chanticleer Lounge, and the mezzanine; today, a large and evidently quite festive convention of ophthalmologists has reserved much of the hotel. Edwin is embarrassed because of his damp clothing and his furtive, abashed appearance, but it is a relief to know, as he threads his way through the lobby, to the elevators, that most of these men are from out of town and cannot possibly recognize him.

In a tubular elevator, three-sided clear green-tinted plastic,

31

Edwin stands in a crush of men, uncomfortably warm and damp, his forehead beading with sweat. The men all know one another, they jab at the buttons for innumerable floors, exchange witty greetings, inquire after wives and children and hobbies, remark upon the quality of the food served at The Summit—the hotel's revolving restaurant on the top floor of the building: some declare it is disappointing, some say it is all right, one cheerful semi-drunken man claims that it is first-rate. Edwin wonders, with a flash of hope, whether Cathleen might consent to have a drink there, or even dinner. It *would* be risky, but on the other hand, as he explained to her so patiently, a hotel near their own homes is the safest place of all to meet, since who among their friends or neighbors would be staying there... ? Their original plan called for a meeting in the early afternoon, in absolute privacy; Edwin had gone so far as to take the hotel room on Monday and "retain" it through Tuesday and Wednesday so that it would still be his on Thursday, though Cathleen objected faintly to his spending so much money; that hotel, she said, is notoriously overpriced. (But he didn't want anything to go wrong. If this meeting with Cathleen failed, he half-thought he wouldn't have the strength to continue with his life; of late, everything seemed to demand such extraordinary *effort*.) And then Cathleen was to leave in the afternoon, in order to be home for dinner; since she went shopping or out to lunch and galleries and volunteer work for the symphony and for Planned Parenthood, or played bridge or attended fashion shows or charity benefits at the Village Women's Club and elsewhere, nearly every day, it would not strike her husband as unusual, her being gone all afternoon. And Edwin, of course, was to stay overnight in the hotel, and go to his office in the morning, and return home as usual late Friday, when Cynthia and the boys expected him. The plan was complicated, perhaps reflecting Edwin's anxious state, but also his concern for the woman he

32

loved—she would be able to pick up the hotel key in a sealed envelope, an envelope addressed to "Catherine Wain" which would be left in "Albert Wain's" mailbox at the front desk. That way, Edwin reasoned, nothing could go wrong: nothing at all could go wrong. But now he wonders if perhaps he couldn't talk her into staying a little longer, having a drink or dinner. . . . He has had no lunch, hasn't even thought of it, a cursory breakfast that morning of coffee and toast, he's suddenly hungry, dizzy and hungry, perhaps a little nauseous, the crowded elevator (why, he wonders, did the architect make the elevators so small, and so oddly shaped; hardly eight men of ordinary build can fit into this thing and one of them, in this case Edwin himself, is forced to crouch in order to accommodate the sloping ceiling) and the jovial whiskey-breathed men and his warm, over-warm damp clothing and the queer sensation, chilling, tickling, like ants, of beads of perspiration running down his back and sides, and the gradual acceleration of his heartbeat as he thinks *Now we're on the 7th floor, now the 10th . . . now we're on the 11th floor . . .* and at the same time, with another part of his mind, he sees vaguely, fuzzily, as if she were a figure in a deliberately unfocussed arty film of the kind he dislikes, his lovely Cathleen waiting for him on the 16th floor, in that room, quite likely standing at the slash of a window, pensive, waiting, perhaps worried about him: all these elements mingle, and clash, and leave him short of breath. Ah, he should have telephoned her from the lobby! One of the hotel phones!

Ophthalmologists from Iowa, Vermont, Florida. From Hawaii. From California, South Dakota, Georgia. Some get off, but unfortunately others, bound for The Summit, push their way in. Edwin sees to his alarm that the button for 16 has not been pressed. He has to request several times that someone press it for him, before he's heard. A tall sandy-haired gentleman in a pin-striped suit and a plaid necktie who resembles—but, thank God, is *not*—a Woodland pediatrician the Lockes know is leafing through a magazine in order to show a companion something, and Edwin cannot resist looking, intrigued by the man's lowly throaty chuckle and his repeated promise *Now this-here is the real thing, I mean this is the real number-one absolute last word thing—* Edwin stares, isn't certain he is seeing what he seems to be seeing, then looks away, shocked, if not shocked irritably surprised, annoyed, he has never been interested in pornography, still less in sick pornography, he finds it difficult to understand, really, why presumably intelligent and civilized men are sometimes susceptible to it. If he had his way, he'd have such magazines banned; their editors fined, or even imprisoned; not only is pornography disgusting and demoralizing but it is pointless, needless. . . . If he had his way even the consumers of such trash would be liable to arrest . . . fines . . . public exposure. . . .

On the 16th floor he forces himself to walk calmly and slowly. Now he is alone: the corridor stretches out before him, lavishly carpeted, decorated with gold-and-black wallpaper, discreetly lit, even a little shadowy in the distance. He wants to rehearse his first words but his mind, his brain, seems to have gone blank; like his mouth it has gone suddenly dry.

1618, 1620, 1622. . . . He has walked a considerable distance before he realizes, irritably, that he is headed in the wrong direction; the odd numbers, 1631 among them, are on the other side; he'd made the same mistake on Monday, and had vowed not to make it again. . . .

So he hurries back in the direction he came, half-running, his briefcase slapping at his leg. 1608 . . . 1602 . . . 1603. . . . By 1615 a man and a woman stand speaking earnestly together; or perhaps they are quarrelling; but they have the good manners to lower their voices as Edwin hurries past. 1619 . . .

34

1625 . . . 1629. . . . Now he forces himself to slow down; he wipes his face with a much-used tissue, and suddenly regrets not having used the men's room off the lobby—why didn't he think of it in time, and why didn't he think of dialing Cathleen from downstairs? At 1631 he pauses before knocking. A silly scared smile slips on and off his face. He straightens his shoulders, he licks his lips, he hears—or does he imagine it—voices inside: she has turned on the television set for company; the poor woman has been waiting for him for over two hours now; he can imagine her distraught expression, her eyes brimming with tears—

He knocks. Quite sharply. And calls out her name. "Cathleen? Dear?"

And after no more than a second or two the door swings open.

III.

The Confession

In the Jade Room of the exclusive Ethel Oliver's shop in Woodland there are innumerable mirrors, a soft plush rug, ceremonial music turned discreetly low, gowns and dresses and suits and negligees with Parisian labels, and Queen Anne chairs for husbands who sometimes accompany their wives and sometimes go alone, to be attended by soft-spoken sales-women skilled in the art of dealing with men who want to buy something for their wives and have no idea what they want, only how much, in general, they want to spend.

There, some weeks ago, Edwin selected for Cynthia, for Christmas, the champagne-colored negligee and nightgown outfit she has rather carelessly, just now, pulled from the hook on her closet door and let fall across the foot of her bed... as she continues to speak in her high, hurt voice, which has always had the power to move Edwin greatly, in ways he does not altogether like, of the inexplicable absence of the Gellers from their party tonight. *Why*, when Carolyn seemed so happy to accept the invitation, back in the first week of January, and when he, Edwin, had the impression from that meeting with Clifford—wasn't it at the Athletic Club, that would have been only a week ago Thursday—that they were both looking forward to the evening, and were cer-tainly planning to come, why, *why* did Carolyn telephone at

37

the last minute—almost literally: at 5:10 that afternoon—to say they couldn't make it after all, something else had intervened, would Cynthia ever forgive them?—and in that soft highpitched little girl's voice she uses when she *knows* she is being outrageous— Why did it happen, why do such things happen, Cynthia asks, her gaze remote, her expression abstracted, as if she were contemplating a roiling chaos of the sort her husband, flat-footed in his stocking feet, his pin-striped shirt partway off, cannot fathom.

Edwin says again, hoarsely, that the evening went well just the same ... didn't it ... ? *She* looked very beautiful, weren't there innumerable compliments on the dinner, and the crepes, and the hot hors d'oeuvres that she worried over, and' didn't it work out well to seat Joe Hanson and Floyd McKay at opposite ends of the table.... Cynthia, her elbows crooked as she unfastens her pearls, makes a vexed face as if Edwin's remarks were distracting her from something more important; for a long moment she stands there, her arms raised, motionless. A strange posture. Edwin, who plans to tell her about Cathleen tonight, in fact in another minute, stares uneasily at her. It crosses his mind that this attractive woman with the stylish hair and the slightly thin, aquiline nose, standing in her slip but still in her high heels, her smooth skin somewhat flushed by the late hour and the drinks she has had, her pearl-pink lipstick eaten partly away, this woman is his *wife:* and how had it ever come about, years ago, that he, Edwin Locke, dared marry her, dared marry anyone ... ? An amazing feat, a prodigious accomplishment, never entirely understood and, until this moment, never entirely contemplated. If he had known what would be required of him ....

She continues speaking, remarking on Gina Henley's weight loss, and that rumor about Charles Diehl and his partner, and the maid's surly behavior—there she was drinking left-over drinks in the kitchen and everything was a half-hour

38

behind schedule and did she even pretend to be sorry, to apologize?—and Edwin loses the train of her words and hears only her voice, her baffled querulous hurt voice. He loves her very much. Has always loved her. Very much. Yet he is going to hurt her in another minute—it may be, he thinks, frightened, that he will destroy her.

I have something to tell you, he will begin. *It's very difficult to find the words to . . . .*

There is no alternative, no recourse. As he unbuckles his belt he realizes that his fingers have gone numb. If he fails to tell Cynthia tonight Cathleen will never forgive him. In the morning he is to call her, at 9:30, to report Cynthia's response; and she will then tell Charles. . . . He had planned to tell Cynthia at the very first of the year, for it seemed to both Cathleen and Edwin that a new beginning, a new year, demanded absolute truth from everyone; and Edwin agreed with Cathleen that the lives they were living—the lies, the petty deceits, the degrading maneuvering, most of all the anguish of being without each other—were contemptible. He had planned to tell Cynthia, had set aside an entire evening to explain, to attempt to explain, but for some reason found himself unable to speak . . . very nearly paralyzed with apprehension; and the next morning he awoke with the flu. You look so sick, Cynthia said, alarmed. Edwin, you look *deathly.*

And now it is January 31. And now he is going to confess. And attempt to explain. And perhaps, perhaps—so he and Cathleen have hoped—a way will be found for them to be together permanently. I love you so much, Edwin has told Cathleen innumerable times, I want to marry you, I want to be with you all the time, is it too much to ask. . . . I love you so much, Cathleen has told Edwin, shyly at first, and then with greater passion, I think I've *always* loved you, since that time three years ago at the Breckenridges', do you remember?—yes, I began to fall in love with you *then.* Edwin's head is filled with Cathleen. His senses reel at times, his tongue is thick and numb, his words come forth vague and half-formed and bewildered. Dreaming. At night, during the day. Asleep. Awake. Cathleen. My love. When are you going to tell her, Cathleen's soft voice demands.

Distracted at work. On the expressway. Talking with his sons, with Cynthia. Approaching his own house—the large gray-shingled colonial with the red shutters, at the very end of Sussex Lane—which has the look, at such times, of being completely unexpected, unanticipated, ownerless. Do I own that house, Edwin thinks. Am I paying mortgage installments on that house. Do I live in it with three people who belong to me, my wife and my children Donald and Teddy, have I just made arrangements to have the slate roof repaired, and must the shutters be painted again this spring, *must* the whole house be painted again, was it worth it to buy a house of real shingles, real wood, instead of one of those cheaper but cheap-looking aluminum places.... Do I own this, do I want this. Do I want any of this.

The Diehls' house, on Fox Pass, in the Sioux Creek area of Woodland, is even larger than the Lockes', a Federal colonial made of stone and wood and white brick. It has three tall chimneys, the Lockes' house has only two.

Cathleen of Edwin's day-dreams; Cathleen on the telephone, in his arms, pressing against him in bed in one of the hotel rooms. Do I deserve her, how can I make myself deserving of her, he thinks.

Is there no alternative? There is not. Cynthia, unsteady on her feet, almost slips on the hardwood floor; she gives the throw rug an irritated little kick. Her high heels are very high. Edwin had, vaguely, not known that high heels were back in style again—he'd thought they belonged to the fifties or early sixties—until he noticed his mistress wearing them: her long shapely legs shown to advantage in them. As Cynthia's legs are also.

"Oh hell," Cynthia says.

"Yes? What's wrong?"

"I broke the catch on this. . . . Lucky I didn't break the string too, there'd be pearls everywhere, that *would* be the final. . . ."

Cathleen on the golf course, that day in July. Cathleen crying, just before Christmas. A mystery. An enigma. That she *talked* so much, and that he *talked* with her, in response to her: while in his imagination there were only, there had always been only, the gestures of love, highly stylized and graceful, and silent. Isn't love most powerful, most pure, when it has no voice, Edwin thinks. For the voice (whether Cathleen's, whether Cynthia's, whether his own) so easily trivializes the soul. *When are you going to tell her. . . .*

The girl Maddie was rude, she "talked back," the agency must be informed. Who will do it: Edwin or Cynthia.

" . . . actually *saw* the ugly little black thing draining those glasses, and do you think she was embarrassed . . . ? Edwin, are you listening . . . ?

"Yes. Maddie. You want to complain to the. . . ."

"*You* should. From you, it will sound more convincing."

"But I didn't actually. . . ."

"Of course you didn't *actually!* Haven't I just been explaining? . . . Look, I'm tired of this. You don't listen to me. You nod and seem to agree but you don't listen, you stand there like a zombie, of course you're half-drunk, you had far too much to drink tonight even after I warned you, you just don't have any awareness of or consideration for. . . ."

She throws the necklace onto the bureau top where it clatters loudly. A frightful sound: Edwin flinches.

Cathleen in a dream just as he awakes, sexually excited, his eyes careening in his head; Cathleen complaining in her high, hurt, breathy voice. You promised to tell her before Christmas. And then it was after New Year's. And now January is nearly gone. Have you changed your mind, is that it, please be honest with me, we agreed we would always be truthful with each other, in the entire world the two of us would be an island, an oasis, of truth, you haven't forgotten?—you haven't forgotten?

It is said that a man measures his age not by his mirror image but by his wife's face. True? Cynthia, frowning and pale, drawn, weary with exasperation, with dislike of *him*, staring at him in the dim light of their bedroom at 1:50 A.M. Lines that run from her nose to the edges of her mouth. Lipstick half eaten away. Mascara and eye-liner weirdly black, too stark, too vivid. "... listening? They pay much more attention to a man's voice, at the agency. I mean to a man."

"Yes, I will. On Monday morning. I will."

"And if you see Clifford...."

"Yes."

Brushing her short wavy blond-brown hair roughly, back from her ears. Looks darker. Their honeymoon: that hotel in Maine, the overcast skies, the drafty room; even in August a considerable chill to the night air; their slight embarrassment with each other, their timid joy. Married? At last? Tense and cautious and solicitous and.... Oh, he had loved her very much. Cynthia. Cyn. He had loved her very much, that girl. Odd, the maneuvering of bodies in a single bed, after a lifetime of being alone, sleeping alone. No wonder he felt obligated to apologize. His body was *large*. His love-making so clumsy. With Cathleen, that very first day in October, the same sort of awkwardness: tender, self-conscious, rushed. Eager. He loved her very much. Loves her. Very much. Now it is January 31 and very early in the morning, in fact it is February 1, it is very early Sunday morning, he is about to clear his throat and say *I have something to....*

Sussex Lane. Not the largest or the most attractive house on the street but impressive: built on a slight knoll, and with that

42

handsome slate roof. Asphalt-topped drive. (But will it need repairs often, Edwin asked, eight years ago, and the real estate agent said no, not often, no more often than any other kind of driveway.) Red shutters, gunmetal gray shingles, a brass door-knocker in the shape of a horse's head. Evergreens, rhododendrons, a single stately oak. (The last elm was cut down years ago. Like a death in the family, isn't it, those wonderful old trees, Howard Maccabee said as the power saw brought it down in pieces, in pieces. The neighbors saved money, had their elms cut down together, the same lawn crew.)

Oh, said Cathleen one afternoon, sleepily, the Maccabees are your next-door neighbors. . . . I like him well enough but have always been undecided about *her*.

"Donald's reading comprehension, whatever that means, precisely. It seems not to be connected with the other."

"Yes?"

"This Hyland I was telling you about, he sounds like a gym coach over the phone."

"Oh I thought—what about Mack?"

"Mack quit! I *told* you. The new guidance counsellor is someone named Hyland, he thinks pretty well of himself, interrupted me in the middle of a question, Don says he isn't too bad but I don't think we're going to get along, I really do think you'd better come with me— I made the appointment for Wednesday at 4."

"But I don't think I. . . ."

"I'm *not* going alone. He sounds like a drill sergeant. Interrupting me, telling me about my own son's—"

To Cleveland? Or Thursday? ". . . on the calendar downstairs, I'm certain."

"Well, I'm *not* going alone."

Cathleen opening the door to him. Her flushed cheeks, startled eyes. Beautiful woman. Beautiful. . . . But we don't know

43

each other very well, she protested. Of course we know each other, Edwin said, gripping her arm. How his heart had swollen! The daring, the risk; the ecstatic joy. On the plane to her he'd read in the *Times* about the kidnapping of a German industrialist, and about the resignation of a British cabinet minister who had been involved, many years before, in the abortion-death of a very young girl: in Parliament the minister had delivered a two-minute resignation speech in an almost inaudible voice and at the end he began to sob and turned abruptly away from the microphone. Had he loved the girl? Very much? Had his love for her been worth the consequences? "Stunned silence" in the vast room. . . . In the elevator ascending to the 16th floor Edwin had seen something very ugly in a men's magazine but he had looked away at once.

He detested such things, he didn't need such things. He pitied the men who did. Who were after all sick, in a sense. Who were sick.

Once, on the telephone, back before the October meeting, the poor alarmed woman actually began to apologize to Edwin. As if she were to blame for his predicament!—for loving her! He interrupted with a despairing laugh.

But we don't know each other very well, she said. Then, later, she confessed: I think I've been in love with you all along. But I didn't quite know it.

Edwin in his pajamas, Cynthia in the champagne-colored nightgown, with genuine French lace around the collar. It might be a little thin for the winter but I don't care, I'm going to wear it anyway, it's so beautiful and I deserve something beautiful once in a while, Cynthia said, a little drunk Christmas Eve, kissing his cheek. Why did she pretend to want to make love, why did she pretend to be hurt when he failed, when he failed, why did she pretend to be disappointed, all those times . . . ? Her relief was obvious. *He* knew. Forty-one years old and forty-four years old which is not, of course, *old.*

44

The kidnapping (and subsequent murder) of the industrialist. The resignation of the cabinet minister. Edwin's knock on the door of 1631 and the door opening and Cathleen there, as he had imagined, as he had dreamt, as he had *willed*. Her hair filmy about her face, her lips trembling, her face so utterly incalculably beautiful.

My love, my dearest Cathleen, my only one, my only. . . .

Suppose you had left?

Left! How could I have left! I picked up the key ahead of time, I've been up here reading magazines and trying to keep from going crazy with worry and then that business about the flight being delayed at the other end and circling the airport here and I didn't know from one minute to the next. . . .

A frenzied embrace. Their hot, damp, flushed faces. Their lips, their vows: I love you, I love you so much, if something had gone wrong today. . . . And, afterward, as he'd hoped: martinis, sandwiches, even potato chips. Room service. And much later, even, dinner at The Summit: how very easily she made the telephone call to Charles, how very easily it was all arranged. Why had he doubted . . . ?

Her "hurt" breast. Which, little-girl-like, she explained to him, she presented to him, with tear-brimming eyes. . . . I was afraid you wouldn't love me. You wouldn't think I was beautiful any more.

My darling Cathleen, my poor girl!—I didn't know.

Not badly scarred. The left breast, the outside. A nonmalignant cyst, it had been, "hardly the size of a peppercorn."
. . . Afraid you wouldn't think I was beautiful any more.

He kissed the breast, weeping. With love. With love.

Odd that the Diehls had declined the invitation to tonight's party. But at least, Cynthia says, Cathleen had the courtesy to decline it right away. . . . Carolyn Geller *is* a very strange woman. Gina mentioned something about their fifteen-year-old seeing a psychiatrist, is there any truth to it. . . . I'm really

45

just as glad they didn't come: you know how Clifford and Joe argue about Medicare.

(An evening in your house would be too torturous, Cathleen said. There were tears like tiny crystals in her lashes. Tears like tiny pearls. To see you there, to see you with *her*, to realize how distant you are from me, really. . . . O my love, am I distant? How can you say that I am distant when I'm with you always in my thoughts!)

The dinner at The Summit very easily arranged. The acquisition of a mistress, the beginning of a love affair, very easily arranged after all. Why had it seemed, beforehand, so difficult, so intimidating? It had taken him so long to get from the terminal to the hotel . . . but if he had the journey to do again, he'd do it in less than five minutes.

Nothing to it, really. No trouble at all.

A pliant woman, Cathleen Diehl, surprisingly insecure. That *was* a surprise to learn. She seemed not to guess at her beauty, her power over him, over men. Her complaints of Charles: sometimes rather bitter. Embarrassing to learn of the man's personal habits, leaving underwear around, excessive drinking, stomach trouble, impatience with Crystal, failure to. . . . Cathleen lying in Edwin's arms weeping angrily: My life with him is hellish. I keep up a good front, don't I. No one has ever guessed. No one has ever guessed.

You'll have to leave him, Edwin whispered.

. . . only my mother. And I *think* his mother. But she's such a selfish woman, even if she did guess she'd never. . . .

Cynthia in the nightgown, rubbing cold cream on her face, quick upward strokes. The hors d'oeuvres did turn out well, at least the girl was sober for the first part of the evening, that's little enough to be grateful for. . . . But the shock of that telephone call! At 5:00 in the afternoon! Two hours before the party!

Edwin clears his throat. Sitting now on the edge of his bed, barefoot, big knobby frightened toes kneading the rug. He says, vaguely, that Carolyn will probably call and explain everything and. . . .

"Yes. Of course. But the damage has been done. I'll never, never forgive her," Cynthia says with a wounded little laugh. "Silly as it all is. Silly as everything is."

Silly?

In the beginning she "forgave" him the incidents, the times when "nothing happened." There was the pretense that she cared, that she wanted him to make love to her; once, she even feigned tears. (Of sexual frustration? Cynthia? It was a ludicrous possibility.) As time went on, as the months passed, it became quite evident that she was secretly relieved; and, after all, in all fairness to her (so Edwin reasoned frequently: in all fairness to her) why shouldn't she be relieved . . . ? He went to so much trouble, made so much effort, mainly for his own pleasure; she rarely responded, rarely took much interest, even in the first years of their marriage she had been shy about such things, or perhaps simply indifferent. It's a hormonal thing, she said. I've been reading articles and it's basically not even a psychological thing, it's just chemical. So you see.

His father's death. Stroke. High blood pressure for so long, what could he expect, why *didn't* he take care of himself. . . . (But he did. He had. Had tried. So Edwin protested, feebly, to his own mother.) A massive stroke, paralysis for weeks; another stroke; and then finally, mercifully, another. Death at the age of 74. Not old by today's standards but not *young* either.

"He had a good life."

"A rich full life. . . ."

Overhearing Cynthia on the phone. Talking to—? Odd if it had been Cathleen. Eight, nine months before the meeting at the hotel. Back in February. Previous year. Ah, a year! Anniversary on the 4th. On the telephone to another woman:

47

Edwin is bearing up pretty well, I think. Of course it was a shock. They say men are liable to cave in when their fathers die, our next-door neighbor Howard Maccabee nearly had a breakdown and how old do you think his father was when he, he was 94! And still. . . . But Edwin has been mature and responsible as always, he's such a *sane* person. . . .

From Cathleen's soft white breast they had taken a tiny lump, a tiny harmless lump. No harm. The scar was not really disfiguring. Though she thought so, seemed to think so. Charles hates it, she said bitterly. I don't believe that, Edwin said. But he won't come *near* it, she said. Well I pity him, Edwin said uneasily. I don't pity him, Cathleen said. I don't feel anything for him at all.

Then we must get married. We must, soon.

When are you going to tell your wife?

. . . and then I'll telephone you. I'll telephone you.

In December, before Christmas. Then you said just after New Year's. And now it's. . . .

But I love you so much. I can't bear the thought of losing you.

. . . now it's almost the end of January, why is it so difficult for you to *speak* to that woman, are you still in love with her, are you afraid of her . . . ?

Charles's vomiting, late at night. In the downstairs bathroom where he thinks he is undetected. Poor man. Ulcers? Nerves? Why then doesn't he cut down on his drinking, wouldn't that be the reasonable . . . .

A rumor, Charles Diehl and his partner Breckinridge. Either an enviable *coup* or disaster. Which? Is there no alternative?

He had a good life. A rich full . . . .

And always so, you know, *sane.*

And once she found a single dirty sock in her clothes closet. In *her* clothes closet. How on earth it got there he couldn't explain, any more than he can explain why his soiled under-

48

clothes are sometimes kicked under his bed or under the clothes hamper.

You'll have to leave him, Edwin whispers, pressing his hot blind anguished face against hers. In the dark they huddle together, naked. Shivering and naked. I love you so much I can't bear the thought of losing you, I want to marry you, it isn't too late, I am still fairly young, once we make our decision the details will fall into place, please don't doubt me, please don't doubt my love. How could you have thought I wouldn't think you were beautiful because of *that*. . . .

No larger than a peppercorn. Only a cyst, a harmless thing. Women get them. Even girls get them. Occasionally. Cynthia too, a sudden scare, examining herself in the bathtub and crying out in surprise and alarm, but then afterward . . . afterward . . . evidently . . . evidently it was not. . . . How long ago? Ten years? Still a young woman then. But.

Is there no alternative? In the dark, in the fatigue of dark, Edwin's eyelids fall shut like dolls' eyelids. Hadn't had too much to drink this evening—in fact had been watching himself—went easy, very easy, on the brandy—two or three martinis before dinner. His eyes fall shut and his jaw, though he is still awake, still awake, falls open. Cynthia's muffled voice. She is the one who drank too much. But would never admit it. . . . Your idea to keep Joe and Floyd apart worked well except Floyd started to pick on poor Martin about that State Attorney-General thing . . . and what was Gina saying to Meredith for so long, right after dinner, I thought it was almost rude the way they. . . .

No alternative, no recourse. He will confess. In another minute, in another minute. His wife must listen to him for once, she must take very seriously what he is going to tell her, both their lives will be changed irrevocably, and the boys' lives, and Cathleen's little girl what is her name, Crystal, so pretty, rather bold and outspoken for a child her age but pretty . . .

Charles must love her . . . must adore her. . . . Children.
Wives. Husbands. Why? So silly. *I have something to tell you,*
Cynthia. It's very difficult to find the words to. . . .

The murdered industrialist. Billionaire, only 38. My age. No
picture of wife but would be of course beautiful: tragic-
stricken beauty. The cabinet minister broken and sobbing. In
public. Before a packed gallery. The hush, the reverent silence.
My own father, when the lightning-bolt struck. *Which he*
never believed would strike. Does your life come into focus,
suddenly and terribly into focus, is there a gauging of the im-
measurable loss, or is it a flood, a bursting, a chaos . . . ?

Or is it merely . . . is it merely something that happens one
day and, in happening, supplants something else?

He clears his throat. There is a hoarse phlegmy rattle in his
throat. A catch at the very root of his tongue, a click; followed
at once by a loud snore. Which wakes him. Which pops his
eyes open. O God the exhaustion. The fatigue. Too much to
drink. Months and months and months and months. *Cynthia,*
he says at last, his voice rising shrilly, strangely, *I have some-*
thing to tell you, it's very difficult to find the. . . .

50

IV.

In The Whale's Belly

On Lurline Boulevard just south of Wainboro Road, in the Westgate Center—a brass-toned building of some fifty storeys set in a field of stubble and mud, surrounded by partly-constructed buildings of smaller scope, and the remnants of woods, and half-razed barns and farm houses—there is a ground-floor pub called The Whale's Belly which, though still smelling of fresh concrete, is darkly cozy, and companionably warm, and frequented by people not likely to know Edwin Locke—office workers, men of indeterminate occupation and income in stylish, cheap clothes, occasional truck drivers, and women who, judging from their monogrammed uniforms, work at LaRue Beauty Salon of the Westgate Center. Here, one rainy April evening at 6:50 P.M., at the imitation oak bar, amid the intermittent rock music from a juke box and the shadowy jumble of decorations—fish netting, corks, lobster traps, plastic sea horses and starfish and mock dragons, and life-sized gleaming ceramic mermaids with hair that looks genuine—Edwin stands sipping a glass of bottled beer and eavesdropping on a conversation at a nearby table. Rise, is that the name? Or Risa . . . ? Hard to hear in the din of music and voices and occasional braying laughter.

Sipping beer slowly. Eating pretzels. It is only 6:50 and he can be home by 7:30 if he leaves in ten minutes and if the expressways are clear—the northbound Ringer, the eastbound

51

Mack—and the rain hasn't turned to sleet or hail. Should telephone Cynthia, perhaps. Before leaving. Work at the office again—that same portfolio that was giving him trouble last week—unavoidable delay—but, yes, the one good thing is that the rush hour traffic will be past, both expressways should be clear. Will telephone in another five minutes.

Risa. He heard it quite clearly that time, and cannot resist looking around. Though he doesn't want to attract the attention of anyone at her table. . . . Risa. Large-boned, tall, with a somewhat broad face, a Slavic cast to the wide-set eyes, lips full and glistening and eager to part into that sly slow red smile. Must be in her mid-twenties. Very pretty. Very sure of herself. Endearing habit, raising and wriggling her shoulders. As if tickled. Loud hearty guileless laughter. And then a fit of giggling. Odd that she isn't with a man but with women. Girls. Office girls? Beauty salon workers? (But they are not in uniform.) Edwin wonders: What are they laughing at, the six or seven girls at that table? Throwing their heads back, shutting their eyes, gay, silly, very pretty, very young.

Sipping his beer slowly Edwin studies her. But covertly. Cautiously. So that no one can see. Her hair is a sunburst of red—red-blond?—that falls wavy and loose past her shoulders, and curls into little tendrils on her chunky breasts. She has a habit of flicking it impatiently out of her eyes, allowing it to slip back, and flicking it out again. Lovely hair. Long and tangled and gleaming, catching the light from the mock lanterns that lean at sharp angles out of the stucco wall, and from the gas-jet fire in the fireplace at the end of the bar.

It *is* the same girl, Edwin decides. The girl walking the dog back in March, over on the Westgate Court Apartments side of the building, three or four weeks ago it must be by now. . . . Fur coat, lynx?—high coppery leather boots, black turtleneck sweater, oversized sunglasses with octagonal frames. Tore off her glove to fit two fingers to her mouth, whistled shrilly and angrily for the Doberman pinscher to come back to her, though Edwin had not been frightened. Nice dog, good dog, he murmured, that's a good, good dog, nothing to be excited about, no one is threatening your or your mistress, good dog, good dog. . . .

Ugly creature, barking and snarling, snapping at his legs. Why had the girl unleashed it, hadn't she noticed Edwin coming from his car? But he hadn't been frightened. Only prudent. Cautious. Afterward when the dog turned away to bound back to his mistress Edwin called out, in a voice that hardly quavered: *Handsome dog!*

The girl in the lynx coat, her red-blond hair partly hidden by a white scarf. Long legs in copper-colored boots. Sunglasses. Red mouth. A coincidence, she'd stayed in his mind and materialized hardly a week later in The Ram's Horn, a popular tavern near the Monarch Life Building, this time in the company of a young man whose face, in profile, showed a beakish nose and a receding chin. And once, here, at The Whale's Belly, late one Friday afternoon when Edwin had felt the need, the desperate need, to get away from the office but *not* to go to The Ram's Horn or the Easy Rider or The Bar where people from Monarch were apt to be, he was certain he'd seen her. . . . The same coat, the same octagonal glasses, seated at the rear of the pub in one of those tiny tub-like booths, holding hands with a man whose face Edwin couldn't manage to see.

Now he knows her first name: Risa. An odd, exotic name, but quite fitting. Quite fitting.

Today, a Tuesday, and a very long one. Should be leaving soon. Time for one more beer, perhaps. Handful of pretzels. Half-stale but tasty. Today: at the office by 8:30, on the telephone to New York half the morning, will have to fly out to Los Angeles at the end of the week, which means the business with Cynthia must be concluded by then. Lunch at 12:15. At The Round Table out on Audubon Parkway, fighting traffic

53

both ways, three martinis, two cups of black coffee, unwise, both unwise; not back to the office until after 3. Business negotiated at the lunch only partway completed; and after he returned to his desk a telephone call undercut most of *that*.

Gas pains. Eerily unsettling.

. . . And Cathleen stroking his warm damp forehead murmuring Please don't shut me out, Edwin, don't shut me out, don't be like *him*. You turn away from me and you're so, it seems that you become so, *tense*, and *interior*. . . .

Another time, with her at The Condor Motor Inn, the very worst time of all, after their quarrel in early February: the terrible jabbing pains, the warning pains, of diarrhea, and Cathleen pressing herself against him, sobbing angrily, accusing him of not loving her, of not caring whether she lived or died.

The time? Not even five to seven. Might as well have another beer.

Cynthia. Meeting him at the Hansons' for cocktails, threading her way through the crowd, smart, pert, self-conscious, in a new Chanel suit and a haircut new that very day, blown-dry, fresh and airy and blond. The evening he had hoped to tell her at last. To confront her. You will have to tell the truth, the frank simple unadorned truth, Cathleen told him. That you no longer love her. That you no longer want to remain in the same house with her.

Cathleen's disappointment, after his cowardice on the very last day of January. In the morning, guiltily, he telephoned her to say in a cracked voice that he'd been unable to tell Cynthia . . . the party had gone poorly, one of the couples hadn't showed up, Cynthia had had too much to drink and was bitter and maudlin and very, very hurt . . . and it hadn't been the right time to tell her. . . . If Cathleen had been present she would have agreed: the poor woman was already distraught, it would have been *brutal*.

You don't love me, she had said. You don't *love* me.

54

Of course I love you but Cynthia is too, Cynthia is, you don't know how unstable she is these days . . . she must sense the situation . . . she is not the woman she appears to be, socially. . . . The party didn't go well last night and she was heartbroken afterward, she threw herself across the bed crying, I'd never seen her so. . . .

I don't care about her! I don't want to hear about her!

But you don't understand. . . . Cathleen, please. *Please.*

After a while she asked who hadn't showed up, and when Edwin said the Gellers she said, *Carolyn* Geller—! But why the hell invite her in the first place?

Tuesday: a very long day. He is so tired he prefers to stand at the bar, if he allows himself to sit he might not be able to get up again, his legs ache, there is a terrible weariness in his bones, in his gut. Tuesday Wednesday Thursday Friday. A call from Cathleen at 11:30 which he hasn't yet returned. (Will say his secretary Trish never gave him the message.)

The only thing that matters, he hears himself telling her, is our love for each other. Right? Our love for each other.

Kissing her damp salt-flecked cheeks. Blowing wisps of hair playfully off her forehead.

Right?

He loves her, loves her. But her moods. Her threats. If you don't tell her I will. I'm not afraid of her. Or of Charles.

Her quirky little fears, charming at first, and then unsettling, annoying: But aren't my breasts too small, isn't the scar disfiguring. . . . I've always wished I had perfectly straight hair. . . . That *she*, Cathleen Diehl, should doubt her beauty, her power over other people, over *him:* it is a revelation, it is a considerable disappointment. I always hated my looks when I was a teenager, she says often, musing, I would have given anything for plastic surgery, or some sort of miracle. . . . My skin was bad too. Don't you believe me? But it was, it was!

A burst of laughter at the girls' table. Risa throwing her

head back, hair an exclamation about her broad strong intimidating face, teeth glistening. No fears there. No uncertainty about her beauty.

Risa in the lynx coat, striding in her leather boots. Cheaply glamorous. Cover-girl-glamorous. Whistling shrilly at the Doberman pinscher whose brown-black snout darted with unaccountable rage at poor Edwin's ankles. Snarling, crouching, ears laid back, ugly bastard, should have kicked in its muzzle, ripped open its belly.

Handsome dog! Edwin had bravely called.

That day, shortly after the violent quarrel with Cathleen, her threats, hysteria. Never had he heard her so despairing, so helpless, so profane. (You lying son of a bitch. Oh you bastard!—fucker!) He had begged her forgiveness, his stomach reeling, guts reeling, aflame. The day that Teddy discovered him on the basement stairs sitting in the dark, tears streaking his face, shameful, hiding, one of his wife's children; and the boy crouched over him and checked to see if he had a fever (the ruse was, had been for some time, "Daddy's coming down with the flu"), pressing his dry warm little palm against Edwin's guilty forehead. Don't be sick, Daddy, huh?—don't be sick, please! The boys love him, evidently. And he loves them. Which makes the situation no easier: which makes it, in fact, much worse.

He will invite Risa out for a drink. Somewhere. Maybe to that new jazz club on Churchill Road, the girls at the office have been chattering about it, art nouveau decor, rather stiff prices but after all he can afford them: and to Risa he will say, My sons love me and their love is breaking my heart, do you understand—my boy Teddy put his hand on my forehead to see if I had a fever and he said *Daddy please don't be sick, please don't die!* And you're the only person in the world I can tell. You're the only person in the world I can share my sorrow with. I can't talk to Cynthia, I can't talk to Cathleen. Never to

56

Cathleen. You're the only person in the world who knows me for myself, who refuses to judge me. . . .

Lobster traps, plastic starfish and sea monsters, mermaids with glinting scaly tails and ceramic bellies and breasts that gleam wetly in the half-light and long languorous undulating tresses. The jarring smoky silence after a rock record ends. The nasal drawl of a man to Edwin's right, perched on a bar stool, one of his elbows unwittingly nudging Edwin's arm. And over to the left and back from the bar a few yards the table of six or seven girls, Risa among them, ordering another round of drinks. (Should he offer to pay? An "unknown admirer"? But the waiter would tip them off, eventually. The bartender, a pal, would tip them off.) Mermaids, breasts and bellies and pert upturned tails. Fish nets. Spears crossed over the archway to the restrooms. Too much smoke. Too much laughter. Strangers' laughter. . . . In The Whale's Belly that day in late February after the disastrous two-hour session at the motel in distant Arden Glen, Edwin impotent for the first time with Cathleen, the jab of a spear through his guts, never to forget, never to forget, and the woman's indecipherable silence: "forgiving," or sullen? or merely baffled? disappointed? bitterly disappointed, like his? (With Cynthia it was usually an almost cheerful *That's all right, dear*, dismissing him, the relief almost audible as she turned aside and he went to his own bed; though years ago, when the bouts of impotence first began, when he first began finding it so *very* difficult to feel what used to be called lust, or even desire, for his wife, it seemed to him that Cynthia had been—hadn't she— somewhat disappointed too.)

The Crusader Motor Inn, Arden Glen, twenty miles from Woodland, one sweaty shameful interminable afternoon. Edwin laboring over his mistress, his mistress laboring over him, feverish, grim, baffled, embarrassed. And silent. For what, after all, is there to say: one cannot crawl those three or four yards into one's own bed, there is no second bed, it is not night, it is not marriage.

Afterward, several hours at The Whale's Belly. Scotch on the rocks. Living and reliving. Seeing again. Feeling. The rubbery limpness, flaccidity, like pieces of celery Cynthia keeps in the refrigerator, gone limp after a certain period of time, irrevocably so. Pieces of celery in a Tupperware bowl. Irrevocably? No alternative? He came here, to this dim smoky noisy congenial place, and got drunk, and resisted a fellow patron's attempt at conversation—You from around here? You live over in Westgate Court, maybe? That evening, no girls, no Risa. The place had been almost empty.

Tearful. Trembling. Despairing. What do I want, what do I really want. The mingled hurt and relief, jealousy and gratification, when Charles insisted that Cathleen come away with him on a two-week vacation in the Dominican Republic. (Crystal was left with one of her grandmothers. Cathleen did *not* want to go: or so she said.) The knowledge that she was gone and would not telephone: a relief at first, and then a gnawing ache. She did, after all, love him. It was love of him that drove her to such excesses. Claiming that he seduced her, drew her into loving him, ruined her marriage, came between her and her little girl. Claiming that he had done these things—he, Edwin Locke!—deliberately. Sometimes I think, Cathleen would say, her lower lip quivering, that only death will give us peace.

Only death.

Peace.

Risa, do you hear? Do you take pity on me?

His father's funeral. Mud that day also. Cynthia, gloved, squeezing his hand. And in bed squeezing his hand. Don't be afraid, it's all right, I've got you, someone has you, it's *all right*.

Except, of course, it isn't.

Risa, do you understand?—*you* understand.

Risa's confidence. Almost intimidating, her mane of red-blond orangish hair, her broad cheek-bones, wide-set eyes. Laughter from deep in her chest and stomach, followed by high tittering giggles and that delicious wriggling of her shoulders: so girlish, so inappropriate, with her large breasts. She is wearing, tonight, another turtleneck sweater. Peach-colored. Rather tight. With several gold chains about her neck, and pendant earrings, easily four inches long. Swinging. Glinting from the gas-jet flames.

Bartender, a word. Come here. A word in private. ... That table there, the girls, there, a free round for all, and no strings attached; an anonymous admirer, that's all. Anonymous. Must be anonymous or the deal's off. Understand?

Understood.

Spear in his guts, in his groin. Shadow falling across their struggling naked bodies.

Of course I love you. I will always love you.

Of course it makes no difference!

But isn't the scar ... disfiguring?

Makes no difference.

Irrevocable. No alternative. *I guess I can't, sorry I can't,* whispered into the dug-out grave, no one to hear.

Look, it makes no difference, things like that make no difference, all that matters is. ...

The slender young man to Edwin's right, matching him beer for beer. No draft, what the hell?—I thought you had draft here.

Must be mixing us up with someone else.

Shit.

The girls at the table giggling. "Anonymous admirer." Can they guess? Not likely. No. He's safe. There are, after all, so *many* other men in the pub tonight, most of them solitary patrons.

59

Risa at the jukebox. Broad generous self-conscious hips. Blue jeans, the peach-colored sweater, shoes with thick five-inch heels. Tall wide-shouldered girl. Mid-twenties, no more. Slight swagger. Is she drunk? Leaning over the jukebox, tapping on the plastic with a coin, fingernails long, polished, as of course they would be. Swallowing, Edwin stares. Stares. The rims of his eyes burn sadly. ... Since he saw her walking the dog over by the Westgate Court Apartments she probably lives there, would be walking back, it isn't far but it *is* dark (what time is it?), she should have an escort. Supposing he introduces himself. The age difference is a shield, a barrier: no danger. I just don't think a girl like you should be walking out here alone at night, he will say quietly and reasonably. It isn't dangerous like the downtown but still. . . .

Or if her car failed to start. Motor whining and failing. Turning over, then failing. He happens to hear, stares over in her direction, frowning, a little vexed because he *is* in a hurry, then calls: Miss, do you need help? Is it flooded?

She slips into the passenger's seat. Deftly, with no fuss, he starts the car. There you are, miss, he says. My name is Risa, she says. Well, Risa, there you are, he says, sliding out of the car. You won't have any more trouble with it tonight.

Or: driving her home in his car. The enormous rich-smelling yacht-like and slightly ludicrous Lincoln Continental.

(Why ludicrous? He was baffled, even hurt, when Cynthia, fresh from her night course—"Contemporary Poetry and the Contemporary Scene"—at the Woodland Public Library first spoke of his car in a gently mocking way. Yes, but why?—why? Hurt at first, then defiant. Why? Because the people who write that trash poetry can't *afford* Lincoln Continentals, that's why, if they could afford them they'd write poems in honor of them, he said scornfully, but his wife had an answer to that: No, if they could afford Lincoln Continentals they

60

would buy Mercedes-Benz, you don't understand poets, Edwin, you don't understand the poetic temperament.)

Risa, however, would admire his car. Would in fact adore his car.

I'm not entirely satisfied with it, he would say with a sigh, but it *does* handle well, the seats are comfortable. . . .

It's fantastic, Risa would say. God. I love it.

The wiry little man to his right has nudged him in the ribs and is evidently speaking to him. In a drunken nasal drawl, one eyelid half-closed. "Hulga Sweet. Name familiar? Sweet Hulga Sweet."

Edwin swallows a mouthful of beer and shakes his head vaguely.

"Rose of Tralee, then, You heard of her, eh?"

No. Edwin shakes his head. Smiling ruefully.

"Moonmaid II?"

Who?

A young-old man. Balding. Quite drunk. Wizened face. Fake-leather trousers (which must be uncomfortably warm in here). Boots with considerable heels. Shirt open to mid-chest, showing kinky black hair. And a chest oddly bony. (Or is he misshapen? He seems, suddenly much too small: hardly Teddy's size.)

"You've heard of Wilhelmina Riley, then!"

"No, I can't say that—"

"Stacey Sugar?"

"I—"

"Rose of Sharon?"

"Are these—actresses? Dancers?"

"These are *horses*, for Christ's sake! I rode them all! Now the slyest most diabolical one was. . . ."

Edwin sipping at his beer, nodding vaguely, in a sudden wild black despair at being trapped in conversation with a drunk while behind him, somewhere behind him, Risa is leaving the

61

jukebox as her record comes on, Risa in her snug-fitting jeans
and her tight peach-colored sweater is sauntering back to the
table, Risa who doesn't know of him, who has gazed upon him
only once for a brief minute or two as her Doberman pinscher
snarled and leapt at his legs and he murmured Nice dog, good
dog, no trouble now, good dog, nothing to be excited about, no
danger, no harm. . . .

Edwin sipping beer, wiping his mouth with the back of his
hand.

A very long day. Tuesday, it is. Is it? Tuesday. Began so very,
very long ago, the alarm ringing at 7, the half-blind walk, staggering, to his bathroom, to the shower stall. The long rainy interminable day. Lunch at The Round Table. Or had that been
Monday? Or was it tomorrow. Scheduled for tomorrow. Wednesday. Round Table, 12:15. Business lunch. At another table
near the salad bar, Charles Diehl and two other men, one of
them a slight acquaintance, attorney specializing in zone-
breaking, land speculation, with a casualness he had not
known he possessed Edwin waved heartily at Charles, grinned
and nodded. So very long ago.

Elfin, leering, the little man with his pot belly carried high,
above his belt, and his spindly arms and shoulders writhing
with excitement. "Hey. Mister. Yes you. C'mere. . . . I seen
you looking at her, the one with all the hair. The one who was
sitting by the fireplace with all that bunch."

Edwin, blushing, cannot resist looking over his shoulder—
but the girls' table is empty. How long have they been gone?

". . . seen you watching her, Mister. How's about a drink, for
a favor? Eh? She's an old buddy of mine, the redhead. Real nice
girl. You want me to introduce you?"

Edwin draws himself up to his full height. "I don't know
what you're talking about. Of course not," he says.

"No? You're sure? You're really sure?"

The little misshapen man has crowded against him, leaning

62

his head around and peering up into Edwin's face. Clowning, acting the buffoon. Edwin steps away, confused. His heart is beating wildly.

"Of course not," he says. "I've got to be leaving anyway."

"Hey. Mister. Don't you at least want to know her *name?*"

Edwin sets down his glass. His face is burning. Is anyone else listening? Is the bartender listening?

"Risa's an old buddy of mine," the little man says, drawling, "and you look like a real gentleman and—what's the harm?—eh? I mean, what's the harm, we're all ladies and gentlemen, school's out, that kind of thing. —Oh hell, shit, if I'm scaring you away, if you're leaving on account of a little friendly chatter: I'll give you her name for nothing, as a favor between strangers, eh? Mister? Risa Allen over in 25-B. Westgate Court. Got it? Risa Allen, 25-B. Give her a ring, tell her Duke says you'll both get along, she'll give a snort of a laugh at first but ten-to-one she'll invite you up. Mister? Got it? How come you're leaving so fast?"

Unsteady on his feet Edwin hurries up the gangplank. The time: only 7:20. Or has his watch stopped? It seems to be much later. Much later. . . . And outside the rain has turned to sleet. April sleet.

V.

The Way

I don't know, I can't predict, sometimes he's reasonable and sort of sweet, other times he explodes without listening to me. . . . He pulled my little finger out of joint once, the bastard, she told Edwin, who reached at once for her hand. And stroked it. A warm dry not-small hand, restless in his, but willing to be stroked.

But you said, didn't you, that he left town. . . .

Oh but he comes back. He's got contacts here. I don't even *know*, all the contacts he has. . . .

If he sees other women, it doesn't seem quite fair that you can't see other men, Edwin said gently.

Oh it isn't! It isn't fair. I know it isn't, everybody tells me, it *isn't*, that's the hell of it. It isn't *fair*. But he comes from this kind of, it's a kind of tradition, a man like you wouldn't even understand, you do things the way they should be done and wouldn't dream of, you know, pushing a woman around. . . . Once he blacked my eye. Well it didn't go *black*, it was just sort of purplish and yellow; and it was only an accident, he was fooling around the way he does, and his elbow sort of. . . . I couldn't go out for three-four days, not even with dark glasses, that was when I worked at Bagatelle, receptionist, you know Bagatelle . . . ? Public relations, they have their office kitty-corner from Monarch Life, the worst thing about that building is a sort of wind tunnel when you walk, you know?—across that big piazza or whatever you call it. Funny, isn't it, that we never ran into each other there.

Yes, Edwin said slowly, it is funny. I must have been distracted. . . .

Of course I looked different then. My hair was sort of red-black, then. Cut short. Curls. You wouldn't have *known* me.

A nervous giggly flick of her hair, back from her shoulders. (It was caught, that day, by a braided green-gold headband that gave her a vague Amazonian look.) Just think, Edwin: we wouldn't have *known* each other then. . . .

Now on a Saturday evening in early June, a warm, over-warm, humid evening, Edwin sits alone in his car, smoking, his eye fixed upon the glaring brass door of The Way, a popular discotheque south of the Bowie Road. 9:30 P.M. He has been waiting an hour. Over an hour. Sadly he picks a fleck of tobacco from his tongue and leans forward to regard himself in the rear view mirror. In the sudden beam of headlights from a car just turning into the parking lot his face has a ghostly, suspended appearance: but he greets it with a feeble warmth, like a brother. Is this a mistake? Waiting for her? But what else can he do? He has been waiting for weeks. In a sense for years. All his life. For her. Risa. Risa Allen. (In the emerald-green negligee and nightgown set he bought her at Sak's Regency Room, her wild hair flung back, her eyes moist and thickly-lashed.) . . . He has been waiting over an hour, she has been in The Way far longer than their plan called for, the man she is with (what can Edwin call him: her former lover, her former friend) promised he would not keep her more than fifteen or twenty minutes. He wanted to see her once again. And she felt that she owed it to him. There's nothing between us any longer, Edwin, she said, but I can't just walk out on him forever, don't you understand? (Edwin answered the telephone at Risa's the other day, when she was in the bathroom, and in a mock-courteous voice the former lover said he only wanted

66

to straighten out a few details with Risa: such as the matter of a certain loan, and his ex-wife's fur coat, and other items of his stored in Risa's apartment for safekeeping. Just a quiet conversation in a public place. No pressure put on her, certainly no scene, who gives a damn—so Pollock said with a contemptuous hissing laugh—about *that* bitch?)

Risa Allen. Edwin thinks of her, and his eyes fill slowly with tears. So much has happened. So very much has happened. He realizes that he is, after a lifetime of illusion, about to break free ... about to discover himself. A frightening process. Terrifying. But necessary. To *know* himself, to *be*. ... I think it all began, Risa, he will whisper, in her arms, lying snug and warm in her arms, that day at my poor father's funeral. I looked up from the coffin and saw these utterly alien faces ... the faces of strangers ... and my vision seemed to darken ... for a moment I thought I was going to faint. Someone squeezed my hand and I wanted to snatch it away. Who were these people, what did they want with me! *I* was not dead. There was a death but it wasn't mine. They seemed to want to make it mine. Do you understand? My dear? My love? Risa? You *do* understand, don't you?

Another car turning into the parking lot. And another. The Way is very crowded every night of the week, it's said, but quite impossible on Saturdays. Why are you going to meet him *there*, Edwin asked, pragmatically, if you want to talk won't it be noisy ... ? Oh it's an old favorite of his, Risa said, shrugging her magnificent shoulders, a sentimental kind of thing, it doesn't mean shit to *me*. A brass door bright as a mirror. Spotlights. Cars parked everywhere. Young men and women in odd, striking outfits, very young, a girl hardly more than Donald's age, in a gold lamé jumpsuit open nearly to her waist, a boy with brilliant red frizzed hair and a lilac shirt and tight-fitting cream-colored pants, faces that float past Edwin's windshield, gay and weightless and insubstantial as balloons, and all so attractive, and all so young. It is bewildering, really, to think of the world filling up rapidly with the *young*.

Earlier today, a wedding at St. Joseph's of Woodland, a high nuptial mass, the bishop of the diocese himself, stately portly mellow-voiced old man, a *coup* for the bride's parents Ed and Het Farley. (Old friends of the Lockes'. Old acquaintances, rather. You're fond of Het, aren't you, Edwin asked Cynthia, and Cynthia said, frowning, It's you who like Ed, isn't it . . . ? Don't you play squash together or something?) The bride and groom so attractive, and so young. The long white gown, a milkmaid effect, demure and obviously costly, the lovely veil, Cynthia staring and staring, perhaps remembering—; remembering.

Hey. Do you realize we've been married one day, Edwin whispered, long ago. *One day.*

A bride of one day!

The hotel in Maine, the yellow Volkswagen that stalled in the mornings, the drafty over-priced room, the four-postered bed, the gigglings and scufflings and damp kisses.

June and weddings. Brides. The groom too looked remarkably young, with his ginger sideburns and pert dark-rimmed glasses. Said to be, however, a graduate of H.L.S., just entering Het's father's law firm in the city. Smug little bastard. Catholic, evidently. Or pretending to be. . . . Isn't it lovely, the entire wedding party, aren't they all lovely, just the idea of getting *married*, one of Cynthia's silly women friends said beforehand, on the walk; so many young people don't seem, you know, to think of it any longer. Such a pity. . . .

Dressing himself slowly and fastidiously, in formal clothes, like a sleepwalker, with a sleepwalker's calm. Another wedding. Whose, this time? The Farley's daughter. (That little girl!) Attending to Cynthia's barrage of remarks and questions. (About his sudden trip, his emergency business trip, to New York City late this afternoon. Isn't it most unusual, isn't

68

it almost freakish, to be travelling on business on *Saturday* ...? And with a strangled sob Edwin replied: For Christ's sake do you think I want to go! Do you think I want to sit through a wedding and endure a reception and fly out to New York all in one day! Do you think I am doing any of this for myself! Do you think if I had a choice I would be living this kind of life! This life! This life you and I have gotten boxed into! And, as if impressed or intimidated by the vehemence of his words, Cynthia remained silent for some time.)

A bride of one day. Risa in the emerald-green nightgown. Tell me about your sons, she whispered, do you have snapshots of them in your wallet? Oh let me see!

In the Regency Room, in the pinkish-golden lights, amid the multiple mirrors and simulated antique furniture and velvet drapes, the negligee and matching nightgown had appeared wraith-like; on Risa, fitted snugly to her full, slightly drooping breasts, it looked brazen and garish, rather like a costume. (It was cut deep in front, deeper than Edwin had supposed. He had *not* intended to buy anything like that.) Oh my God, Risa said, tearing the package open like a child, what *is* it ...? Oh my God isn't it beautiful! It's fantastic. I love it. It's *just* the right color.

A tall big-boned girl. Not plump, certainly not fat; but fleshy. Full. He adored her pale green eyes, set wide in her face; he adored her high-colored complexion; her full moist lips. When she smiled, slowly, revealing her teeth, slowly, Edwin felt a pang run through him—he wanted to laugh aloud, he wanted to sob, she was so beautiful. And so guileless. Self-conscious, coquettish—and yet guileless, innocent. *She knows me,* Edwin sometimes thought giddily.

Ah, that day back in winter!—whistling for the dog, cruelly and coldly *indifferent* to poor Edwin's fear. (Though really he hadn't been afraid of the dog, he had been certain it wouldn't bite.)

69

Risa, do you remember walking that Doberman pinscher, and you let it off the leash, and it ran barking at a man?—just outside your apartment building?—in March? You were wearing your lynx coat, unbuttoned. And a black turtleneck sweater. And leather boots. And slacks. The dog ran at a man and began yipping and snarling, and you whistled for it to come back, and— Yes? You do remember?

Oh that wasn't you! she whispered, staring at him through her outstretched fingers. Oh my God that wasn't you!

Kissing and cuddling and tickling. Snug. Warm.

Honeymoon.

Whose dog was it?

Some man's.

Yes. But whose?

Oh some man's.

What were you doing with it?

Taking care of it. Dog-sitting.

But why? Where was the owner?

Oh out of town, I think Barcelona. Something about buying a factory there.

Barcelona?

Yes, isn't it in Spain?

Where is the man now?

Oh he's back, I don't know where he is now. He paid me to take care of the dog. Dobbie. I got to almost like him, after a while. The thing about Doberman pinschers is, they're very *sweet*, but they have bad reputations.

Was the man a very close friend of yours?

Oh no. No he wasn't, actually.

And your other friend—Pollock—didn't care?

He was in Tokyo. Actually I think they know each other.

But he didn't mind?

Are you interrogating me, Edwin? I don't like to be interrogated.

70

Shaking her hair irritably out of her face. Turning away.

Don't be angry, dear, he whispered.

St. Joseph's. Stained glass windows: pale yellow, dark green, red, a bright brilliant turquoise blue. Wealth. Altar of ivory and gold. White roses, mums. The bride's mock-modest gown. Her bowed head, her gleaming hair. Groom's tuxedo. Groom's sideburns. So young. Bastard. Het and her son-in-law, flush-faced, being photographed. The bridesmaids. Simpering. Ed Farley's aged mother in a wheelchair, legs atrophied, thin as sticks, terrible to gaze upon. Photographed. The booming commandeering voice of the wedding party organizer. (A portly young man not in a tuxedo. Said to be high-priced but efficient.) The Farley-Davenport nuptials. Society page, next week. Big spread. Wealth.

How has it happened, Edwin asked Cynthia, that the Farleys have invited us? A high nuptial mass—what does it mean? They know we're not Catholic.

Don't be ridiculous, Cynthia said, you don't have to be Catholic to attend a wedding.

It isn't just a wedding, it's a mass. Do we have to kneel? How long will it last?

Catholic services are very beautiful, Cynthia said. My college roommate was Catholic and I went with her once or twice and . . . and I was very impressed. But the mass was said in Latin then.

Oh. And this won't be?

They speak the vernacular now.

Thinking of Risa all along. Sweating, and thinking of Risa. In the car amid Cynthia's perfume and chatter (why, oh for Christ's sake why, does she chatter so much these days), dreaming of Risa with her wild hair and chunky breasts and soldierly stance, out on the walk, her leather purse slung over her shoulder. I don't like to be interrogated, Edwin, she said curtly.

71

A shock through the center of his body.

Thinking of. Dreaming of. At a traffic light, sitting uncomfortably in the pew, listening to the bishop's high womanish droning voice. Do you take this woman to be your lawful wedded . . . . Risa? My love? I didn't mean to offend.

The delirium of love-making, with her. With her. Pleasure so keen it unnerved him, stayed with him for hours, diffused in his body, in his blood. Oh I love. Love. You. This.

My bride. Squeezing my hand. Someone has you, has you, don't be afraid.

The Catholic nuptial mass. Less exotic than he had supposed, but unpleasantly long. So long! (Stealing a forlorn look at his watch. And where is Risa now? They are to have dinner together at Viktor's and then he will drive her to the discotheque off Bowie Road where she will meet, for the last time, Da Vinci Pollock, her former friend.) . . . Chanting, singing, music, stained glass windows, statues of Mary and Joseph and Jesus Himself, life-sized, in pastel colors. Not of ceramic but of a material with a slight glaze; subtly yellowed; perhaps they were genuine works of art from Europe, perhaps they were clever reproductions. Edwin's gaze wandered restlessly about. The flower-decked alter was gorgeous, the bishop's gilded costume was gorgeous, there was nothing to offend the eye here, for even the outlay of wealth was in good taste. How much, Edwin wondered idly, had gone into . . . well, for instance, the women's hair-dos . . . and it looked as if a fair number of the men had had their hair professionally styled for the occasion too. How much money? Thousands of dollars?

Risa too. Expensive tastes. A $40 hair-do that lasted one day; a $400 suede pants suit was too tight in the crotch and consequently never worn; the little Fiat she is currently begging for. Child-like in her crudity, her silly innocence. She would not understand the restraint of beige, off-white, dove

72

gray, the deceptively plain bride's and bridesmaids' gowns, the understated magenta of the bride's mother's gown. She too would have been restless, forced to sit through an interminable ceremony on a fine warm June day. . . . Playfully, daringly, he would squeeze her thigh. Here. Right in church. And she would slap at his hand, snorting with laughter. Hey! What the hell! This is a holy place, Mr. Locke! . . . Sometimes I wonder, she would say drily, just what kind of person you *are*, Mr. Locke.

Not known. Not to any of you.

Secrets within secrets.

Intriguing, though. His and Cynthia's numerous Catholic acquaintances. You steer clear, of course, of all embarrassing difficult subjects, you never speak of birth control or abortion, should women be allowed to become priests, should priests—should nuns!—be allowed to marry; and of course it goes without saying that you never allude to religious experience itself, or to God. (How on earth, at a Woodland party, could one talk about *God*, Edwin wonders with a smile. The awkwardness of it!) Unless you learn, of course, that they are "liberal" Catholics. Which seems to a non-Catholic a contradiction in terms: but let it pass, let it pass. . . . But there can be, occasionally, a sudden unanticipated union arising from mutual amusement and contempt toward "conservative" Catholics: for instance Woodland's highly vocal crusading Pro-Life group, which sponsors heated debates on abortion in area high schools, on local television programs, at the Village library and the YM-YWCA, and which continues to attract a fair amount of publicity. Fervent people, Edwin thinks half-enviously. Such *belief*. Such *faith*.

The enigma of Catholics: clinging to a truth, their truth, in the face of (perhaps because of: so it seems to an outside observer) that truth's improbability. Perhaps, Edwin wonders as he uncrosses his legs in the narrow pew, and glances again at his watch—so little time has passed!—they somehow *tested* themselves; took it as a measure of strength to see how much they could retain of their childhood faith even when it became quite obvious that the faith itself was child-like, a child's vision of the universe? He could respect that position, in a way, though he could not quite understand it.

Heaven and Hell and Purgatory. Saints, a Saviour, a beginning and an end to time, the dogma of elderly Italian men, an eager adoration of riches in various forms. ... He would squeeze her thigh boldly, brazenly. Right here. While the bishop droned on and the young couple knelt in their handsome costly outfits.

Risa has, so far as Edwin knows, no religious beliefs at all. She has not repudiated them—she simply has none. A dim notion of "God" that is roughly equivalent to "Fate"—*Well that's the way things go*, she says often, glancing at the newspaper's headlines (flood, earthquake, Mid-eastern crisis, Ford workers laid off, Washington figures exposed in scandal), switching from one television newscast to another. Edwin finds it endearing, her indifference to—or is it an unawareness of—what might be called a larger design, a continuity, a causal pattern. For instance, the future: does it exist, will it exist? Since the age of twelve Edwin has been worrying about the future. His grades, his performance in junior high school, high school, college, graduate school, in his first job, and in his second, and in his third. ... He began at a certain point, some years ago, to worry about his sons' future; and to "worry," in a manner of speaking, about the future of the United States, which had always seemed to him, previously, unneeding of any private citizen's concern. By contrast Risa worries about money, but only about certain sums of money: the price, with taxes, of a new coat or a new dress or a new pair of shoes. "How much" something costs is than translated into "how long" it will take to acquire that sum—which is what Risa

74

knows of the future. She is also capable of thinking of "next weekend" and she will sometimes mention "next winter" (when—it is hoped—they will be able to spend two weeks together, in Jamaica), and Edwin has heard her speak, sometimes with a small sad smile, of "someday"—which she often modifies, her smile turning droll—"someday when I'm rich and famous." And her friends, those Edwin has met, are even more child-like than Risa: they drop in at all hours, they fly to California on forged credit cards, they beg, or bring, marijuana, hashish, beer, liquor, even (though rarely) cocaine; they arrive at Risa's apartment without warning, just back from an eight-month hike through northern India, sleep four and five to a bed, express cheerful gratitude but not much surprise when Edwin sends down to Tin Roy's in the Westgate Center for a dozen Chinese dishes. And the telephone calls! The bill for long-distance calls alone. . . .

Risa in the low-cut green nightgown, smiling slowly. Flicking her hair off her shoulders, drawing in her breath. Risa in the lynx coat, two impetuous fingers to her mouth. (Was she whistling for the dog, or for Edwin? How he would love to ask her!) Risa in the scarlet shirttail shirt and the fashionably baggy unpleated skirt, tonight, a menswear bow tie at her collar, her hair, newly tinted, supplemented by a crazy, charming wiglet that is all curls and frizz, her long wide feet squeezed into high-heeled shoes that are nothing but straps, so improbably fragile—so fashionably "feminine." Risa kissing his lips. Hurrying away. Teetering in the shoes. At the glaring brass door, turning to blow kisses to him, knowing he is watching, knowing he is staring, in love, in love.

In love. For the first time in his life.

Had she known, back in March, when the Doberman pinscher rushed so noisily at him? Snapping, snarling, barking. Yipping. Ugly brute, its bulging mad eyes slightly crossed, or so it seemed. Had she known who he was, how he adored

75

her, what he would willingly suffer for her . . . ? A beautiful impetuous woman, leash in hand, fingers to her mouth, whistling. I adore you, poor Edwin wants to shout, but cannot be heard over the noise of the dog's barking.

The creature *is* barking. Angrily. Insanely. Why doesn't it leave me alone, why doesn't the son of a bitch quiet down, if only I had a stick or a gun, if only I had a gun. . . .

Barking. Yipping.

But—

No, wait.

Edwin shakes himself awake abruptly. Someone is shouting. Where is he, what has. . . . He is sitting in his car, someone is shouting nearby, he remembers, he remembers what the situation is, and knows even before he gets out of the car that the quarrel involves Risa, and that she needs his help.

"Oh no you— What do you think you— I *said* I had more to—"

"Stop it— You bastard, let me—"

"You goddam fucking lying bitch—"

Bravely Edwin throws himself at the man who is struggling with Risa. This is evidently Da Vinci Pollock, with whom he has spoken on the phone several times, and it is a surprise—he hasn't time to register it as a halfway agreeable surprise—that Pollock is shorter than he, and obviously very drunk. A young-old face, furious, distorted with fury, a beakish little nose and an ugly little mouth and a weak little chin— impossible to judge his age though he is, Edwin supposes, considerably younger than he—and amazingly strong—quick and strong and *certain*—perhaps he is accustomed to such things, sudden shoving matches, struggles, shouts and curses, sudden fights, exchanges of blows with strangers, in the beam of headlights someone has turned on so that a small circle of onlookers can better see what is happening—

Bravely Edwin Locke takes on Da Vinci Pollock in the

76

parking lot of The Way one Saturday night in June. Though he has no time, of course, to think of himself as brave; he has no time to think at all. His only words are: "Don't you dare t—"

VI.

Squid

One cool Saturday night in October, in the crowded living room of Floyd and Una McKay's house on Hawthorne Drive, a somewhat drunken Edgar Hockney, the investment broker, his right foot still in a cast as a consequence of a water-skiing accident the month before, is saying to a skeptical Meredith Platt and several others, ". . . serious. I am. I've seen them. Right in Miami Beach I've seen them. These poor pathetic old people, elderly retired people on pensions . . . just wandering through the supermarkets looking at things, looking at things they can't buy. . . . I mean it's a grave situation. It's a shame. I've *seen* them. Then in the check-out line they're there with the things they can afford finally, like beans and Wonder Bread and dog food, only you know, you know damn well, the dog food is for *them*, I mean it's a phenomenon that has actually been reported on, and commented on, I'm not making it up. . . ."

"Now I have to disagree at this point," Meredith Platt says. "I have to disagree, Ed. My own father is retired, and—"

"Now wait just a minute, please," Edgar Hockney says. "I wasn't finished, wait just a—"

"My own father is retired, he's sixty-eight years old, his pension isn't anything remarkable but he owns his own house and he goes out to dinner anytime he wants and he *won't* take any money from me, let me tell you—"

79

"Meredith, your father was an executive—"

"Ed, look, his pension is very small, very modest, believe me, and you don't see him moping around supermarkets and buying dog food."

"Now wait. Wait just a minute. I may not be able to express myself very clearly but the point is, this is a very serious problem, this is a very tragic situation in the United States, you can deny it if you want and get some cheap laughs, Meredith, but the thing is—the thing is, there are these old people, they really exist, they live in little rooms and flop houses and places like that, and they're so poor they can't buy meat, they are forced to buy dog food—"

"Hey you know what: they buy that for their dogs, Ed. You ever think of that? For their dogs, their pet dogs, there's all these poodles over-running the nation, you ever think of that?—they're buying the goddam dog food for their goddam dogs that are *hungry*."

Edgar Hockney ignores the laughter and says, waving his drink, "Just a minute. That's cruel. You know—that's a cruel cheap very ignorant statement, Meredith. That isn't funny, Meredith."

"I didn't say it was funny, I just said they're probably buying the dog food for their dogs, you ever think of asking them?"

"I just don't happen to think that's funny, Meredith."

Una McKay drifting by, checking on her guests, says in a little-girl voice, "Now Edgar, what are you being so *adamant* about, maybe those people buy dog food because they *like* it—"

Edwin joins in the laughter. He is eager to laugh, to enjoy himself, after all it is a Saturday evening, the first time he and Cynthia have been out together in weeks, he *will* enjoy himself.

"I just don't happen to think the subject is funny," Edgar says, his blunt-boned face creased with vexation. "I just don't—I just don't happen to *think* the subject is funny, that's all."

"Oh Edgar, you take everything too seriously since your accident!" Una McKay says, squeezing his cheek. He has a high-colored, rather coarse, but not unattractive skin; about Edwin's height, with wide, sloping shoulders and the beginning of a stomach. An acquaintance of the Lockes' but not really a friend; and not their broker.

"I'm just making the point that I don't necessarily happen to think the subject is *funny*," Edgar says angrily.

But he has lost the attention of the little group. Someone backs away, ostensibly to freshen his drink; Una is pulling Tyla Hanson off to meet the chairman of the board of education, a woman in a smart tweed pants suit who has just arrived, alone, at the party; cagey Joe Hanson pretends to be interested in a framed splotch of grays and olive-greens on a nearby wall; Edwin adroitly avoids Edgar's bloodshot outraged gaze and turns casually aside . . . and goes to join a boisterous group at the front of the room, by the McKays' grand piano, encouraged by their barks of laughter and by the fact that neither Cynthia nor Cathleen is among them.

He sips his drink appreciatively. It is his second, or third. He nods at remarks. Makes remarks. Joins in the laughter. His eye wanders, his expression is placid, congenial, hopeful. A Saturday night. The McKays' party. A clear bright moon. Lovely. October: lovely. The McKays' warm pleasant familiar living room. Good people. All of them good people. It will hurt him to leave them—it will hurt him very much.

Difficult to make friends at his age. Or is that an overly pessimistic idea.

Risa: beloved and wife-to-be *and* friend. All the friendship he will need.

The thing is, Edwin thinks vaguely, there is little in the world of value except hope. You've got to have some reason,

81

after all, for crawling out of bed in the morning, don't you. So look: philosophy and religion and all the books in all the libraries and all the preachers' harrangues begin with that. Pity bores like Hockney haven't grasped that first principle.

Cynthia, drink in hand, standing with the little balding toad-like man who runs the art gallery in the Village, what is his name, can't recall, something repulsive about him, though probably he is nice enough—eager to make friends, eager to be taken up by people like the McKays and the Lockes. Cynthia with her new haircut, extremely short, gamin, blond, roguish. Handsome woman, isn't she? Well perhaps. A new sternness to her jaw, a new smile. Bright-skinned. Gay.

I don't believe this, she said.

Standing with her arms folded strangely. Not beneath her breasts but across them. As if she were very cold.

I don't believe the things you're telling me, she whispered.

But then, only a few minutes later: Oh I knew. I knew. I knew all along. I *knew.* Your lies and your excuses and your—your absent-minded insulting *selfish* behavior this past year—

Cynthia sipping her drink, sucking at the ice cubes. But mustn't let her see me watching. The veil dropping over her face, that expression of startled dislike, the sudden jowlish bulldoggish look....

And Cathleen.

Not in the room at the moment? Not in the room. Must have drifted into the foyer, talking with someone out there. A blessing, so many people.

A blessing.

Edwin finishes his drink and goes to get another. No point in waiting for the McKays' waiter to happen by; a too-courteous light-skinned black with eyes Edwin is able to read as mocking, even malicious. Make his own drink, why not. Perfectly capable. ... Charles Diehl is at the bar, dropping ice cubes in a glass. Laughing and talking with a man named Smith, golfing companion, no one Edwin can be expected to know. They exchange greetings. Shake hands. How is business? Any trips in the near future? How's the family—Cynthia and the boys? Still playing squash?

Trips: he flies to New York about once a week now, Edwin says, it's tiring but necessary. And he does accomplish a great deal. There is the possibility of a trip to Munich later in the fall. And one of the girls in the office, Edwin hears himself saying, suddenly, she's in Marrakech right now with a friend, another girl, doesn't that sound like an ... doesn't that sound like an interesting vacation ... ?

If Charles Diehl and Smith with his silly little moustache think this is odd information for Edwin to offer, they give no sign. They smile and nod and sip at their drinks and one says he hopes to get to Morocco sometime, before it's too late, and the other says he hopes to get back to Kyoto sometime, he has such fantastic memories of Kyoto.

Edwin asks, curious: What kind of fantastic memories? I've never been to Kyoto.

So the evening unfolds. It is not so exhilarating as Edwin had hoped but it is better, far better, than another night at home. After all, these people are his friends; these men are his brothers. In a sense. Charles Diehl laughing, his head flung back, his glistening teeth exposed: a man Edwin supposes he has wronged, and toward whom he feels some guilt, and a queer pang of affection. But of course he doesn't know, Edwin thinks. She threatened to tell him but didn't.

Another drink?

The McKays' party, first weekend in October: the date circled in red on the downstairs calendar. Something for Cynthia to look forward to. And for Edwin also, though he would far rather—of course—be with Risa. (But Risa is in Marrakech for three weeks. With a girl she'd known as far back as junior high. So she has said. A photographer's model. A very nice girl though somewhat "unstable." Would Edwin mind if Risa flew to Marrakech with an old friend?—would Edwin mind lending her some money? *Hey. I'm going to miss you,* Risa whispered.)

Another party next weekend. And the following weekend as well. And the Breckinridges mentioned something about a New Year's Eve party, though it is hard to tell if they were serious, or just thinking out loud. Red circles on the calendar. A future he shares with his wife. And Cynthia too has been planning a dinner party, mid-November perhaps, and maybe an open house around Christmas since they owe so many people. They have been falling behind in their social responsibilities. . . . What do you mean you want a divorce, you want to marry someone else, Cynthia said, staring, ashen-faced, what do you mean, for God's sake what are you saying, we have a *life* together, we have children, we have the house and commitments and . . . and a future. . . .

I am in love with another woman. I don't want to hurt you but I am in love with another woman.

In love in love in love in love with another woman.

You want a divorce? You want to marry someone else?

No, it isn't possible. He runs a hand through his hair and sighs and freshens his drink. . . . I realize it isn't possible. It isn't feasible.

(The boys. The mortgage. Repairs that must be done on the roof and the furnace. Trading in the second car for a new station wagon. Joint properties and investments and savings. I realize it isn't feasible, Edwin says, sickened, staring at his wife's haggard face. A shared life, shared friendships, in-laws, plans for a vacation home in the northern peninsula, inextricable, irrevocable. Social engagements well into December. And of course the boys, the boys. Whom Edwin loves very much.)

If you aren't able to think of me ... at least think of *them*.

I have been thinking of them, Edwin says with a sob.

If Smith weren't here. If he and Charles were alone. Out on the McKays' glassed-in porch, perhaps. Someone to confide in. Someone to ask for advice. ... I know it's crazy but I have fallen in love with a beautiful young woman and she wants to marry me and I want to marry her. I've told Cynthia. She forced it out of me, I told her everything, I want a divorce and I want to marry another woman and ... and it will come about, won't it? Won't it? She loves me very much and I adore her.

Edgar Hockney pushing his way to the bar. Red-faced, visibly perspiring. Something aggressive about his limp. Excuse me, he says, without looking at Edwin.

Drunk.

In love in love in love. With another woman.

On the basement steps, in the dark, he sat. Monday evening. Five days ago already. Sucking at a can of warm beer. Thinking of Risa, dreaming of Risa, murmuring, groaning. (They had had one of their little quarrels. Not about her trip to Marrakech—he was reconciled to that, and even happy for her. Enthusiastic. Be sure to send your lonely lover post cards, he said with a wink. No, the quarrel was about something else, a more serious matter. When he telephoned she often did not answer and it was because, wasn't it, she was not home: she was out with (please don't lie!) another man. Yes? And who was the man? Or men? *Please don't lie.*) After the scuffle in the parking lot of The Way, after Edwin woke in Risa's apartment the next morning, after his tearful proposal of marriage and her acceptance of the proposal ... well, hadn't he the right to assume, wasn't it his prerogative ... ? She had promised to be faithful to him, hadn't she.

On the basement steps, in the dark. Sitting. Muttering aloud. *Not* hiding from Cynthia, as she later accused him. Just sitting there. Thinking. Remembering. Risa in certain postures. Her breasts skimming his eager face, her belly damp and slick, tendrils of her hair in his mouth, stinging his eyes. Her bucking heaving coy body. Her panting, her sly smeared smile. *I love you, only you. Only you.* When the telephone rang she tensed but did not answer it: and he felt at times a thrill of triumph, of possession, as if the caller could see them in each other's arms and know that Edwin Locke belonged with her now, and that everyone else was displaced; but at other times he felt a pang of dismay, sensing how her thoughts flew from him, though she lay with him her thoughts scuttled away and were free of him and his valiant exertions. . . . *But I love you, you know that. Don't be silly!*

Beautiful girl. Fleshy buttocks, breasts. Calves that shone with muscle. Fine glowing skin. Marvelous hair. And her eyes: her lovely eyes. (Quite by accident he had discovered a slight, a very slight, imperfection. Despite her strategic mascara and eye liner and blue-green eye shadow it seemed that one eye, her left eye, turned a little inward, oh just a fraction of a fraction of an inch, and her gaze turned inward; a secret she was loath to admit. Did she, at one time, wear corrective lenses? Had contemplated an operation, even? . . . But the effect is charming, really. Everything about her is charming. She does not exactly know that Edwin knows, now, and it would be clumsy of him to mention it, but when he sees her peering and squinting in her compact mirror, applying eye-liner to direct the viewer's gaze away from the offending eye, when he sees her grimly going about her task, he wants to seize her shoulders from behind and nuzzle her neck and say I love you, I want to marry you, let there be no secrets between us. . . .)

Quite by accident Cynthia opened the door and discovered him there and gave a scream. My God, Edwin, what are you— What are you doing—

One of the beer cans clattering to the foot of the steps.

What are you doing here sitting in the dark!

86

His fright nearly as great as hers. (For he had thought she was to be gone most of the day—a bridge luncheon at the Village Women's Club and some sort of charity bazaar afterward.)

His pounding heart. Sudden shortness of breath. In the ugly brazen light she switched on, so impetuously, his face must have shone blotched with tears. And guilt.

Most astonished of all, her whisper: But why aren't you at the office? *Why aren't you at the office?*

So it came out. His love. "Another woman." His not wanting to hurt "you and the boys." At last it came out. A stammering speech he had rehearsed many months ago, in the days of Cathleen Diehl, now burst from his lips. As he stood, there, on the basement steps, half-crouched, disheveled, reeking of beer (for when Cynthia opened the door and surprised them both he spilled beer on his shirt front), and his pale amazed terrified wife loomed over him. One of the most terrible moments of my life, he thinks, though he later amended it, in Risa's protective arms, *One of the most profound moments of my life. When truth at last asserted itself.*

And so. It came out. All—or nearly all. Last Monday. As he spoke, blubbering, hiccuping, it seemed to him—they were now in the kitchen—that Cynthia was strangely sympathetic; she was actually *listening* to him for the first time in many years. Perhaps the word *divorce:* rehearsed so often but never spoken aloud. Divorce. Divorce? Another woman. Marriage. Remarriage. But oh my God, my God, he sobbed, quite sincerely, rubbing his knuckles into his eyes, I haven't wanted to hurt you . . . it's been hell, to think of . . . of hurting you and the boys. . . .

She had listened. Leaning against the counter, as if faint.

I don't believe this. What you're saying. I don't believe it. You're drunk. Why were you hiding there on the steps, in the dark, why aren't you at the office, it's only 3:30, why are you home, why are you home so early, what is going to happen to us!

Cynthia, please— If you only knew how hard this is for me—

His wife, staring at him. His wife in a smart tailored suit the color of crisp autumn leaves, from Edith Oliver's, a silky beige blouse, an orange scarf tied gaily and fashionably about her neck. His wife. This woman was his wife. Is. *His* wife. The fact struck him like a blow. *His wife.*

You're insane, she whispered. Drunk.

Cynthia—

For the past year you've been acting crazy. You haven't been normal. Absent-minded, drinking too much, staying away for hours, hardly talking to the boys, hardly aware of how much Teddy needs you, and I need you, never listening to anything I say—

I'm sorry. Please believe me when I—

But why are you drinking like this!— in the middle of the afternoon! *Why are you home from the office so early!*

It came out. In fragments, in bursts of emotion. He told her about his love for Risa and she seemed to be listening, she seemed to hear, yet in a brief while she would revert to her original question, her face now shining with tears, her pretty little scarf untied: What struck her most was the fact that he wasn't at Monarch, he was actually *at home*, sitting in the dark on the basement stairs drinking one can of beer after another.

It was that that frightened her, Edwin saw. He wondered if it should frighten him also.

But. So. At last. He confessed at last. And she *seemed* to comprehend. But it was a trick. For suddenly she began to scream at him, she seized something on the counter—the big wooden salad bowl—and threw it at him, screaming, her face distorted and ugly. And he backed away. Quite alarmed he backed away. No, please, don't, don't do this, what if the boys

88

hear, what if one of them comes home, please, no please Cynthia—

(In the end he fled. Fled her hysteria. The scene had been worse, even, than the ugly scene with Cathleen back in— when had it been?—April, May?—that he had made every effort to forget.)

"And how are things at Monarch?"

"Fine. Really fine."

"Cynthia says you've been flying to New York practically every week—"

"Yes. But I get work done on the plane."

"Howard, now, they've been making him fly to Dallas and he has a tendency, I don't know if he's ever told you?—to be plane-sick, and it *is* hard. But once he's sick, he says, he can get work done too. On the plane, in the taxi, in the motel room, he even takes it with him into the dentist's office, and into the dentist's *chair*—we go to Dr. Thayer in the Renaissance Building, you know, he's a marvelous dentist but awfully slow and exacting—has a patient in each of his four little rooms and goes from one to the other and it *can* take a while before you're out—so I suppose it's the practical thing, to take work along—but, you know, I wonder if you're the same way?—I just get so *nervous* in a dentist's chair, my hands go cold and I sort of freeze up—are you the same way?"

"No. I mean yes."

"Poor Howard, I wonder if he's told you about this new program they've instituted at SKT, *Drive to Excellence* it's called and I think it's terribly competitive, and you know Howard hasn't been well...."

No. Yes.

And across the room, deep in conversation with Joe Hanson, there is Cathleen herself; whom he must avoid; if, discreetly, he can; so he is trapped here with Howard Factor's wife, good-hearted, graying, made excitable by alcohol, given to

89

plucking at his sleeve, emitting gusts of perfume and talcum powder.

. . . In the dentist's chair. Thirty-five floors above the Ringer Expressway. Risa's dentist. The morning after. Emergency. A cheerful clucking totally bald Iranian, shorter by several inches than Risa, a neighbor at Westgate as well as a friend, Sure I will do this favor for you, it is no difficulty, will you play nurse for me?—assistant? Here, in this white cap. Ha! Isn't she a beauty, Mr. Locke! Nothing quite like it! You put this thing in the man's mouth, my dear, ah but not so hard, it will cut into his flesh which is soft there—you see!—you can hand me those things—on the tray, yes—it's fun, eh?—like on the television—the big beautiful girl dressed up like a nurse in something white and a cap, eh!—so much fun. Now Mr. Locke, I understand there was an accident, a bad accident, last night, which is a pity, you see the tooth must come out, you see—sorry!—how it wobbles—and I am afraid the adjacent one as well—but it can be done very quickly, it is not so big a project as filling a cavity—and the false teeth, well, just one or two like this is no trouble, you will see. But that cut above your eye! Poor man! What if—what if, you know, it had gone lower? Poor man.

The fight with Da Vinci Pollock, it's said, lasted no more than thirty seconds. Which Edwin found hard to believe. One of The Way's security guards ran over and shouted for Pollock to stop. (What had he been doing? Kicking Edwin in the face? In the belly?) And so Pollock walked off unharmed and got in his car and made an obscene gesture at Risa and whoever else was watching (not Edwin: he was unconscious, lying on his back in a fairly muddy place, his face bleeding from several deep cuts) and drove away; and Edwin was helped, eventually, to his feet, and back to his car, which Risa was able to drive, sobbing and muttering: Oh I'll make him regret this one, the little son of a bitch, the little fucker, this is one trick he isn't

90

going to smooth over. . . .

At Risa's. His face washed. Gargling to get rid of the vomit taste. (When had he vomited? He couldn't recall.) Undressed by Risa who was still half-sobbing. The telephone rang. Rang and rang and rang. And Risa shrieked: The little fucker, listen to him, he actually thinks I am going to answer that, he actually *thinks* . . . ! Undressed. Given a shot of brandy. Lying on the sofa. His shoes pulled off. Dizzy, murmuring, his face and mouth numb, the pain suspended, at a distance. Risa will you marry me. Oh I love you. Love you. Will you marry me, my dear. Be my wife, my dear. Oh please. I have wanted to ask you for many weeks and now I must speak.

In the morning, shy as a bride, in the green negligee, she fixed her blurry slightly cross-eyed gaze on his as he squeezed her hands to implore her, Please marry me, I will tell my wife about us tomorrow, I will call her now if you want me to, whatever you say, whenever you want, please marry me, say yes, the financial situation will be difficult but not impossible, oh Risa please—

His mouth now beginning to throb. His entire head.

Through it, however, through the din of pain, he managed to hear the girl's hesitant answer: Well I suppose I *could*.

"How is . . . how is Crystal . . . ?" Edwin heard his voice inquire falteringly.

Cathleen's words are coolly spaced. In her ankle-length dress of heavy cotton, with her peasant's shawl, oatmeal-colored and -textured, and her antique brooch, she stands erect and composed; her ironic amused stare is fixed to his. Crystal? Oh fine. They had a marvelous birthday party for her last month. Twenty little girls! And all so pretty. And, and. And. She is taking ballet lessons now. At the dancing school in the Village.

"You are? She is?"

"*She* is. I think I'm rather too old for that sort of thing,

91

now."

Expecting him to protest? But, nervous and baffled, he stands mute.

Cathleen with her somewhat droll dry smile. A grin trapped in a lady's decorous smirk. Odd, he had never noticed it before, never in the years of their acquaintance, in the homes of one couple or another: a woman whose beauty, minimal enough, and conventional enough, is swallowed up in irony. For hours tonight they have been avoiding each other, discreetly and imaginatively, and gracefully, Edwin thought, like partners in a dance, a stately minuet; now, as the party nears its conclusion, she has violated the space between them. Why, he can't guess. Why. After their agreement last spring. Why, since she detests him and he fears her. (Fears her wrath more than he fears Cynthia's, in fact.)

Vague forced talk of mutual acquaintances. The strain of pretense. Did he know that Alexander Aulk who used to be at Monarch and left for SKT had a heart attack, only forty-four years old. . . . Did he know that Charles might be shoulder-tapped for a position in Boston. . . . Did he know that the Breckinridges' marriage is in serious trouble. . . .

No. Doesn't know.

Cathleen standing well back from him. Discreet distance. Her smile forced. Perhaps trembling. (*He* is trembling. For no reason. Hadn't they agreed last May, was it, after the outburst of shouting, the woman's ugly accusations, after he had seen *all*. . . . After he had turned aside from her in revulsion.)

Yes. Maybe Boston. Of course it would mean leaving our friends here . . . uprooting ourselves. . . . Wrenching ourselves. . . .

Boston?

His voice flat, unconvincing. Better that, however, than showing the relief he feels. Boston. The Diehls gone from Woodland, and out of his life permanently: so that he never has to *look upon* them again.

"Well. That would be a pity. But . . . . But if it's a very attractive offer. . . . "

"Yes. That's right."

". . . would be a shame to pass by. . . . Opportunity. . . ."

". . . *would*. Yes."

Edwin does not want to think, does not want to think, of what Cathleen's reaction will be when she hears. When news of his and Cynthia's divorce makes the rounds. And news of his remarriage. (They have decided to tell no one for a while. Not even their families. Because—and this is pitiful, pitiful!—poor Cynthia has the misguided idea, which Edwin has encourged, that *perhaps* he can be talked out of "such a drastic move.") Ah, he does not want to think of his former mistress's wrath.

Her distorted tear-streaked face. The blur of mascara, the sudden coarseness of a flushed ruddy skin. Unforgettable. And the ugly *words* that issued from her. Words he could not have imagined Cathleen Diehl *knowing*, let alone *using*. . . .

And the maniacal desperation in her body, and the fury with which she raked her nails across his shoulders and back. . . .

Of course it had been a mistake to agree to see her. "One last time," she had begged. He should have known the meeting would be disastrous but by then—late April, early May—he was so wonderfully in love with Risa Allen that he could not *quite* believe in Cathleen Diehl's existence.

Is it some other woman, she wanted to know at once.

Some other woman! Edwin stammered, as if the very idea were unthinkable, preposterous. But. . . . You must know. . . . I. . . .

It's just your wife, then. Dear sweet stubborn smug Cynthia.

Yes. I mean, I thought we agreed. . . . I thought we de-

93

cided. . . .

We *did* decide. I did. Not to take that shit from you any longer.

Then. . . . Then why. . . .

In the Pisa Motor Inn on the Bowie Road, halfway to the airport. A room on the second floor, smelling of disinfectant and rug shampoo. Daylight. Harsh unsettling daylight. Though their meeting was "only to talk one last time, in privacy," Cathleen pulled the heavy green drapes across the wall of windows, exasperated when they did not quite close. A shaft of sunlight fell onto the rug. These damn drapes, why don't they close, Cathleen half-sobbed, tugged at the cords, what if someone walks by on the ramp outside and looks in. . . .

I think it's all right, Edwin said uneasily. I don't think anyone could really see in. I mean, the crack is only an inch or so wide. . . .

Cathleen threw the cords toward the wall, in disgust.

Everything goes wrong, she whispered.

There had been telephone calls. And letters—five or six letters. Discreet enough. Not hysterical. Not exactly accusing him. A tone of—how could it be described?—for he fully intended to tell Risa all about it, about poor Cathleen—half-hurt half-curious *interest*. I simply want to know, Cathleen said. I simply want to know how you feel now, what thoughts you've had about us, what you think went wrong between us.

What went wrong. Between us.

(What *had* gone wrong? He couldn't remember. The whole thing was a blur, a blank.)

In the Pisa Motor Inn. One Tuesday afternoon. Spring. An attractive blond woman and a fairly attractive dark-haired man. Talking. Talking earnestly. Sincerely. Hadn't they decided it was for the best, Edwin murmured. Their spouses. Children. Oh yes, Cathleen said, lighting a cigarette, no one

94

could be hurt. We knew that all along. We *knew* that along along. . . .

A pity, Edwin thought, he hadn't brought along a bottle of Scotch.

A pity, he thought, as Cathleen talked at length, he had allowed himself to be coerced into this. (And at the back of his mind Risa waited. Beautiful guileless arrogant Risa. How she would roar with laughter if she could see poor Cathleen's strained face, the foolish tears that are about to spill over onto her cheeks. . . .)

I could use a drink, Edwin said.

But so softly Cathleen did not hear. Nor did she pause.

. . . love, for the first time. I know, I know . . . ! So late in my life! But. But it had to be. Now everything is altered. As you know. You saw something in me Charles has never seen, no other man has ever seen. . . . You *can't* retreat and leave me alone for the rest of my life.

What? Edwin asked.

You heard me.

I. . . . I didn't quite hear you. . . .

Staring at him. Her breath coming in long shuddering gasps.

Who is this woman, Edwin wondered, *why am I locked in this ugly room with her. . . .*

And then, somehow, somehow it came about, he was never able to understand, afterward, how it came about—nor would he want to explain to Risa—she had shoved herself into his arms. Somehow, somehow. He hadn't known it would happen. Sobbing, clutching at him, kissing him: Cathleen in his arms, suddenly. She was telling him that she loved him, no one but him, that she didn't want to live any longer, without him . . . he couldn't mean it, could he, when he agreed so blandly to her suggestion that they break off their relationship. . . .

Clutching at him. Kissing. Her intensity, her desperation.

95

What could he do? You are my love, the distraught woman whispered, you alone are my lover, you *can't* leave me.... And somehow it came about that they were half-undressed. And then they were undressed. And in bed together. ("One last time," the woman was begging.) And though Edwin dearly wanted to make love to her, if only to silence her, to contain her, he was quite incapable—quite impotent. And she sobbed, and writhed, and pressed herself into his arms, and ground her teeth against his, and began to rake his back and shoulders, half-consciously, with her hideous sharp nails, and at first the pain was so overwhelming he could not really feel it; then he grabbed hold of her wrists and pushed her from him.

Oh I hate you, she screamed. You bastard! *You!* I wish you were dead! I wish you and I were both dead! And she managed to free one arm, and slashed at him again with her nails, catching him this time in the underside of his jaw, and in his chest. I wish you were dead! You! *You!*

What was happening? He was bleeding from a dozen deep scratches.

He struck out at her, whimpering, and scrambled to the foot of the bed, out of reach of her nails. She shouted: I could kill you! I could kill you! Terrified, short of breath, Edwin Locke stared at the madwoman who lay squirming and kicking on the bed and saw that she was no one he knew—no one he really knew.

Afterward, of course, he was to forget his terror.

Poor man! He was to forget the clarity of his terror in that moment when he gazed upon me, without recognition.

The McKays' party ends abruptly.

Edgar Hockney, staggering drunk, shamefully drunk, imagines that he sees something in a corner of the dining room.

At first he laughs hysterically, then he begins to sob. It's a slug! It's a squid! A giant squid! Can't you see it! Oh there it is—there it is quivering, trying to go up the wall! Stop it! Don't let it by me! It's coming at me! Help! Stop it! Help! Help!

Babbling like an infant. His mouth a torn gaping hole.

Help me! Help me! Don't let it come any closer!

His wife Florence and the McKays and Charles Diehl give him aid. Lead him away. Away. He is babbling, wailing. Poor man. Poor silly man to drink so much.

". . . shouldn't drink so much," Edwin says, starting his car, "I mean with a drinking problem like his. . . ."

Cynthia says nothing.

He drives slowly along Hawthorne Drive. Toward home. A lovely autumn night. Late. Crisp clear marvelous night. Where is the moon?—ah, there. If only Risa were with him. He clears his throat and says, conscious of the sobriety of his tone: "It's a shame about Hockney, collapsing like that. Imagining he saw—what was it?—an invisible shape coming after him—"

"A squid," Cynthia says.

"Yes?"

"A squid."

"Very sad. For his wife too. And for the McKays', their party ending so—"

Cynthia says nothing.

Then let her sit mute beside him. He does not care; in fact he is relieved. In a few weeks he will be free of her, of the oppressive tiresome boring weight of her, and he will never again hear the reproach in her voice, and never again see the puffy "hurt" look she is so expert at contriving. And Cathleen too: he will never see her again. Hateful woman. Repulsive. After that experience in the Pisa Inn. . . . After his humiliating impotence, and the bestiality of her need, her hysteria. . . .

97

Risa, he whispers, I want to be saved from them. Both of them. Oh please please save me! My love.

Turning from Hawthorne Drive onto Siskin Pass. Nearing Sussex Lane. Dark quiet mysterious streets. Lovely. The taste of the air—lovely. If only Risa were with him. If.

But she *is* with him, in a sense. He carries her image everywhere. Let his old wife sit mute and sullen and half-drunk and haggard, a strand of hair fallen across her forehead, let her sit self-consciously in opposition to him, why should he grieve, why should he care? He has forgotten the subject of their conversation. He has forgotten her. He knows only that the October night is beautiful, that the future lies all before him, rich with the surprise, the continual shock, of sensual pleasure; it lies in wait *for* him. The past does not exist. The past is falling away, moment by moment, helpless to impede him.

Risa, my love— My only love—

He floats free of the others. A man's drunken terror, a woman's rage, another woman's cold anger: what do they matter to him? They have no power, they do not even exist. He is free of them. A stranger to them.

To awake! To live! To plunge forward bravely, even recklessly, into the life that was meant for him all along: *this is why we are born*, Edwin Locke thinks, as he turns onto Sussex Lane.

VII.

Game

"Is the chicken dish hot enough?—it seems a little cold—"

"It's O.K."

"... more rice?"

"No thanks."

"What's in here—oh, the shrimps with lobster sauce—don't you want any?"

"I had some."

"Don't you *like* the dinner, Donnie?"

The boy, bent over the tray on his lap, blushes slightly; but whether it is with irritation, or embarrassment, Edwin cannot tell.

"The sweet and sour pork is delicious," Edwin says coaxingly, spooning some of the concoction onto Donald's plate, "why don't you—"

"I *had* some, Dad. I don't want any more."

"Are you worried about the time? We have plenty of time."

Donald shrugs his thin shoulders. "... kind of a long drive," he says.

"Well it isn't snowing. The expressway is dry."

Donald says nothing. But he has always been a quiet child, even a stubborn child; perhaps his odd stiff distracted behavior tonight is not significant. Edwin, smiling at him, wonders what he is thinking. Of course he cannot ask, he dare not ask: since the Great Quarrel with Cynthia in October he has become accustomed to thinking of the boys as his wife's pawns, his wife's weapons, his wife's innocent dupes . . . they are *hers* temporarily and if he wants to win them over he must be very, very careful. And even before the trouble with Cynthia, Donald was a problem. In a manner of speaking.

". . . usually more reliable, this particular Chinese restaurant. The Red Dragon. Maybe you noticed it when we drove in . . . ? I send down for meals two or three times a week, it's much better than frozen food and of course I don't have time to fuss around in the kitchen. . . . The annoying thing about fancy meals," Edwin hears himself saying with a low amused chuckle, "is that you're expected not only to eat them but to applaud them, and if you don't . . . if your mind is elsewhere, for instance on your work . . . you get into trouble. I mean with the cook. I mean. . . . " His words trail off. He isn't certain what he means; why he drifted onto this subject, which seems only tangentially related to The Red Dragon and the cooling, rather tasteless food before him. (*Is* the food tasteless? He can't judge. The martinis have dulled his appetite, and since this morning he has been taking, on the average of one every two hours, throat lozenges, in an effort to forestall a sore throat, and possibly the flu, and for some reason—for some perfectly idiotic reason—the lozenges are heavily dosed with sugar; so all day he has been swallowing a sickish medicinal syrup that has had the effect of destroying his appetite.)

Donald. His son. A slender boy, thin-armed, thin-necked. Now thirteen years old. Sprinkling of pimples on his forehead. Edwin's dark hair, Cynthia's close-set features; but he takes after neither of them so far as Edwin can judge. (He takes after you, Edwin, his mother once told him, nudging him, whispering gleefully, out of Cynthia's earshot; but though Edwin humored his mother at the time, some years ago, he did not really see much evidence of himself in Donald. Which was, perhaps, part of the problem.) . . . Awkward conversation since he picked Donald up to bring him to the apartment. Very awkward. Edwin knows enough not to query the boy about his mother—the one thing he has vowed *not* to do is manipulate the boys' emotions, as Cynthia is doing cruelly and shamelessly—but everything he asks, no matter how peripheral, how innocent, seems to swing back to her. If he inquires about Teddy, about the station wagon and the repairs on the roof and the garbage disposal unit that was to be replaced weeks ago, if he even asks his usual smiling "How are things going?"—a perfunctory but genuine question he has put, over the years, to innumerable friends and acquaintances and business associates and girls at the office—it suddenly seems that he is pumping the boy for news of *her.* Which of course he isn't.

Awkward. Even their remarks about the Place Rivière Towers, and the view from Edwin's apartment on the twenty-third floor. (He thought Donald would be impressed. Which perhaps he was. The view overlooking the Arnason Expressway to the north, and the immense Lurline G.M. plant to the east, with its eerily flickering lights and the rim of flame about certain of its smokestacks, *is* impressive. Though Edwin would have preferred an apartment on the other side of the building overlooking the distant river.) The boy is evasive, cautious, maddeningly quiet. Is he this way, Edwin wonders, at school? Or does another Donald blossom forth? . . . Thirteen years old. Would he rather be going to the basketball game with friends? With a girl? *Has* he friends, *has* he a girl? It doesn't seem quite possible to ask though Cynthia would not hesitate to poke and pry and interrogate, and no doubt has. Edwin stares at his son and the boy raises his eyes to him and Edwin smiles in embarrassment, and the boy glances away, shyly.

"The view is much better with the lights off. Let me just—"

In the December twilight a ceaseless stream of headlights.

101

Far below. Something peaceful, soothing, about it. Could stare and stare and stare, sipping a drink. For hours.

He freshens his drink. Speaks of the advantage of living so close to the office. That commuting drive!—all those years! Breaks a man's back, erodes a man's spirit. The first few weeks—Donald probably knows this—he was sharing a larger apartment with Irwin Lembke not far from the Skyline Mall—Irwin Lembke: the Lembkes live on Indian Village Pass, they have a son but he's, what is he, maybe eighteen, so probably Donald wouldn't have run into him—the Lembkes were never exactly friends because Cynthia disliked Sylvia for some reason, *why* Edwin didn't know, you'd have to ask her—well, anyway: Irwin Lembke who worked for Standard Oil—they shared an apartment until Lembke ran into trouble at the office and got sick, got very badly sick, and disappeared for over a week—frankly he went on a bender, no other way to express it—and Edwin moved out, as soon as he found this apartment, and has been *very* satisfied with it so far. Sometimes, of course, as Donald might have noticed, the wind manages to get through the cracks by the windows so it's somewhat chilly, and in a really bad wind the building seems to move, to sway, but it isn't a dangerous thing, all high-rise buildings—does Donald know?—yes?—all high-rise buildings sway. To some extent. Yes, he is very satisfied with it. "The view alone is worth the price," he says, and Donald does not contest the fact.

He goes on to say expansively, in the slightly fey, "wild" tone that Risa sometimes inspires in him, that there is something genuinely transcendental in living so high; something elevating to the spirit. Just being so far above the ground . . . having this kind of aerial view of the expressway . . . and even, at this distance, the Lurline plant has a kind of . . . has a kind of strange stark industrial beauty. Of course, he says, sipping at his drink, you must have the necessary *eye* to see such things.

Donald says nothing. Edwin turns to him, and immediately the boy murmurs an assent.

"Living in a single-family home, that kind of life, the conventional way of . . . well, of settling down . . . buying a piece of land, you know, and a *house* . . . mortgaging your soul for thirty years . . . not to mention the taxes even after you've paid off the mortgage! . . . taxes forever and ever. Well. That's an entirely different way of life, you know. I mean it's different from . . . from this. I mean, there's no value judgment implied, I don't mean to say, to imply, that. . . . Of course it can get lonely here. At times. In fact I'm not here that often. There's always the element, you know, of the *new* . . . the newness. . . . Like the expectation you have when you enter a hotel room. The novelty of. . . . Well. I'm glad you like it here because you'll be coming to visit and it *will* be more comfortable when I get more furniture. Though it's sort of fun, isn't it, eating off trays? And with this stunning view. I wonder if the erosion of American *vision* doesn't have something to do with people sitting trapped around conventional tables, sitting there trapped for hours and years and lifetimes just staring at one another, with no comprehension of . . . of the great world that awaits outside. Anyway. It's something to think about, eh?"

Donald murmurs in agreement.

Edwin sips at his drink and stares at the view and tries to think, tries to think, what to say. There is something vexing here, something nagging. What is it. He strokes his chin uneasily. Before picking Donald up he shaved, and gargled with Listerine, and made certain that he was impeccably dressed—for Cynthia with her cruel cold unsparing eye would notice any defect. He hasn't been sleeping lately, his stomach is easily upset, in fact it is almost constantly "upset," something he must learn to live with; perhaps when the problems

103

with Risa are entirely straightened out, and of course the divorce itself. . . . The New Year will be a comfort, no doubt. Just the idea of tearing off the last month of this tumultuous year and throwing it away. . . . Crumbling *December* in his hand and dropping it into the. . . .

Donald, his elder son. Whom he loves. (But of course he loves the little boy too. Despite Teddy's refusal to see him, and even to talk to him on the phone.) And in a way he loves their mother. Because . . . because she *is* their mother. And he loves them. And so of course . . . in a manner of speaking. . . .

"You know, I do love your mother," he says suddenly. "I love you all. I . . . I love you all."

"Okay," Donald says at once.

"I mean . . . I really *do.*"

Donald says nothing.

"It's hard for you to understand, maybe, all the upheaval of these past weeks, but . . . despite your mother's accusations . . . the things I know she has told you and Teddy. . . . Despite the things she has tried to poison you with. . . . I do love you, Donald. You and Teddy and, yes, Mommy too. It's just that. . . . "

"Okay," Donald says softly.

". . . just that the human soul requires so much more, so much that can't be . . . that isn't. . . . It's like the view from this tower, I mean this building, if you contrast it with. . . . Well, what was I. . . . There was a point I wanted to. . . . "

"That's okay, Dad."

Groggily he wonders if the boy will report to Cynthia and will get things wrong. Distort his meaning. Misquote. . . . There was always been something sly, even malicious, about Donald. Oh not really!—not anything serious, not a psychological defect. Not that. But something, well, mischievous. . . . The time when, dropping off to sleep in his study, Edwin was awakened by a blaring just outside the door: Donald's trombone, which he was forbidden to play after his

104

father came home from work, and.... Well you could say it was a joke, a prank. Or you could say it was something more serious.

Mischievous, sly. Malicious? Hard to know. (So he has told Risa frequently. A tragedy of life that one's own children are so hard to know.) ... Teddy, now. Teddy is the exuberant sweet uncomplicated one. Or was. Until this sick business about refusing to see or even talk with his father. Cynthia says he won't even talk *about* his father. Which is sick. Which is very serious. *What if that bitch has convinced Teddy that I'm dead*, Edwin has said, weeping in Risa's arms, *what will I do to combat her....*

Edwin must explain something. Before they leave for the basketball game. About love. The definition of. The tragedy of. But it is difficult, very difficult. His throat is sore. His tongue feels numb. The magnificent view of lights, headlights, sparkling tinkling quivering pulsating lights, has turned his mind into ... into a nervous trembling jumble of.... It *is* a magnificent view. Worth the exorbitant rent. And that criminal lease he was forced to sign. If Cynthia could see it for one moment how impressed she would be, how jealous, she would realize he has grown beyond her irrevocably, and that her silly accusations and demands and threats can have no power to....

"Love is.... Love isn't.... What I'm trying to say, Donnie, is that.... Well...."

Love. I love you, Risa, for Christ's sake you know that, he shouted the other day over the phone. Then he wrote a little note on the card he wanted to send with Teddy's birthday present, I love you a bushel and a peck, but it all became rather confused ... because he wasn't sure that Teddy would understand the allusion; though of course Cynthia would. (Wasn't it one of their pet songs in the early days of their marriage....) To both their lawyers, his and hers, he has said in a

105

toneless sober voice that he simply no longer wants to live with that woman, he has outgrown her, he has outgrown the marriage, brutal as it might sound he is incapable of summoning up the strong emotions she evidently still feels for him. *Love.* Love in all its forms. Poor Cynthia's rage, her frenzy at being rejected, left behind, her desire for revenge. . . . He has made, Edwin thinks, every attempt to be fair to her, to be neutral. He refuses to *judge* her. But the situation, exacerbated by her irrational charges, is so dizzyingly complicated. . . . "Love is, well, more than just people feeling that they have to live with each other. It's also a kind of. . . . It's a. . . ."

"Yeah. Okay, Dad," Donald says.

Edwin goes to the kitchen to freshen his drink. There is so much, so very much, to say. His hands are trembling. Perhaps he is coming down with the flu, which would account for his uneasiness, his sense of unreality. Though it would violate their agreement he might telephone Risa before he and Donald leave for the game.

Love is also, he thinks, returning to the darkened little living room, love is also *respecting* one another's differences. . . . Allowing one another space to grow in, freedom. . . . "Are you finished with the food? Do you want anything more? Another Coke?" he asks. There comes a time in a man's life, he will tell his son, in a person's life, that is, when . . . when it's necessary to. . . . And of course his own experience has been immensely complicated because he has fallen in love with another woman. A lovely young woman whom he, Donald, will like. Very much. And *she* will like him too; and Teddy—of course she will like Teddy. And. . . .

But he still loves his family. His sons. Nothing on earth will change that. Nothing.

He sits on the sofa beside Donald and continues talking, grateful for the boy's attentiveness. Maybe the most impor-

106

tant thing he can give his sons, he thinks, is a respect for the truth, a sense that the truth *must* be faced; because it is only through acknowledging the truth that . . . that one alters, grows. . . .

Risa, her name is. Risa Allen. Someday (perhaps soon) the three of them will go out to dinner together. To a show if anything decent is playing. (There are the Twin Cinemas over at the Westgate; very convenient parking.) Donald and Risa will get along very well, they are two of the dearest people in the world, two of the people Edwin loves most in all the world, of course they will like each other a great deal. . . . Risa has asked Edwin not to telephone her for the rest of the month but since his son is here in the apartment with him *at this very moment* that would seem to constitute mitigating circumstances. . . .

But: what time is it?

"What time is it?" he asks, blinking.

He switches on the light and stares at his watch. Going on seven-thirty! And the basketball game began at seven!

"Jesus. We'd better get going," he says, standing, setting his drink down. "We'd better. . . . It's a bit of a. . . . Look, Donnie, why the hell didn't you say something? Were you just sitting there blanked out, not thinking about the time at all . . . ? *You're* the one who wants to go to the game, after all, it's your school and your team and. . . . "

"It's okay, Dad," Donald says in a faint polite neutral voice. "We can be a little late, it's okay."

□ □ □

An enigma, his son. His own son. Thirteen years old but what does that *mean*. It will be ironic that before his separation from Cynthia he never seemed to have time to become acquainted with Donald—for one thing his long hours at Monarch kept him away from home, not to mention the fre-

107

quent business trips—but now that they are separated, now that he is living away from home, he and the boy will have an opportunity to learn more about each other. Over the weeks, the months. One of the ironies of my situation, Edwin will tell friends. When I actually lived under the same roof with the boys I never seemed to have time for them, but *now*. . . .

Though they are considerably late for the game, a number of others are late also, and a small rowdy gang of boys and girls Donald's age, or a year or two older, are milling in ahead of them. Edwin smells, but does not comment upon, the familiar sweetish odor of marijuana. (Should he be shocked? In a way he is. But he thinks rather helplessly of Risa, his mind reverts to Risa, and for a few seconds he halfway forgets where he is.)

Donald is walking a few feet ahead of his father, impatiently, his hands thrust in the pockets of his jacket. Edwin almost hesitates to address him for fear the boy will refuse to answer. (Then he *was* angry about being late for the game. But why on earth didn't he say something instead of allowing Edwin to ramble for so long. . . .) A blond girl detaches herself from the group she is with, and walks beside Donald, exchanging a few words. *Her* hands are pushed in the pockets of her jacket too. Edwin notices, suddenly very interested, that she is an attractive hoydenish girl, maybe fourteen years of age, and how charming, how charming, the way she teases poor red-faced Donald by nudging him with her elbow, as if they were conspirators; she has no awareness of Edwin close behind them, and is consequently behaving in an utterly natural, spontaneous way. Just as she would do during school, in this same corridor. . . . What is she saying, as she smiles so broadly? What does Donald reply? The poor kid is so timid, so clumsy. Edwin hopes the girl isn't contemptuous of him.

"Donnie, aren't you going to introduce us?" Edwin asks.

Blushing, not looking at either of them, Donald introduces Edwin and the girl, whose name is Fran, Fran something. She is less pretty than Edwin thought but there is something fetching, something decidedly striking, about her small pert monkeyish face. Crimped blond hair that looks as if it were tinted. A pale, somewhat mealy skin; but a pair of bright eyes; and a gorgeous smile. Her shoulders are a little rounded, but Edwin notes that many of the young people stand that way. Her voice is nasal but cheerful, mock-courteous. *Hi, Mr. Locke. You guys are smart to come late, somebody said the game stinks. We're behind thirty points or more....* She isn't wearing jeans like the other girls, but black satiny slacks, tight about her small waist and buttocks. Her khaki-colored jacket is lined with imitation fleece. Her vinyl boots are badly stained with salt.

Edwin half-wishes the girl would sit with them, but she rejoins her friends, and he loses sight of her once they are inside the overheated gym, climbing the bleachers. One of the penalties of coming late, Edwin thinks, is that they have to sit at the very top of the bleachers where the air is especially hot; and the climb leaves him somewhat out of breath.

Basketball. Noisy game. Applause, shouts, boos, good-natured insults. Cheerleaders in blue jumpers and gold blouses. Almost too cute. Indeed, too cute. Edwin prefers little Fran with her sly smile and soiled-looking complexion. ... He scans the crowd on this side of the court but can't locate her.

How well does Donald know her, he wonders.

Hard to believe, with that fascinating *look* of hers, the knowing self-conscious sauciness of her grin, that she is his son's age. But perhaps a year or two older. Hard to judge. They wear make-up at any age and at the same time their voices are so high, so child-like; deceptive. Edwin asks, "Is Fran in your class?" but the basketball is being dribbled toward this corner of the court and his question is lost in a sudden din of shrill cries.

109

An enigma, his son Donald. But perhaps any son is an enigma. Any child. He showed so little interest in getting here, and now he is sitting forward, his elbows on his skinny thighs, watching the game with great interest. He too shouts, though rather self-consciously: Hey! Come on! Come *on!* Cupping his hands to his mouth. His entire body shaking with the effort of his enthusiasm.

Thirteen years old but what, precisely, does that mean? Who are his friends, does he have a girl? Does he "like" a girl? Probably not: too young. Too young for that sort of thing.

Though Edwin can remember himself at that age. Or was it even younger. . . . Certain obsessive images, certain shameful obsessive habits. . . .

Donald, however, seems very young. Despite his height he is really a child. And, like a child, he is annoyingly self-absorbed so long as he wants to be. An observer, glancing at Donald and Edwin, would not readily assume that they are father and son, nor would he assume that they are at the basketball game *together*. They happen to be seated beside each other, that is all.

Edwin clears his throat and makes a comment on one of the better players, a red-headed boy in a blue uniform who has just successfully made a foul shot. Donald nods. A few minutes later Edwin asks if Donald might have preferred to sit with those boys and girls instead of with his father . . . but Donald doesn't hear the question and it seems pointless to repeat it.

Or would he rather sit with the girl.

Too noisy to talk. Cheers. Shouts. The game is not, perhaps, hopeless. . . . What time? Edwin checks the clock, prominently on the wall, and his own watch. Oh still early, still early.

He is sucking another lozenge. The warm consoling effect of the martini is still with him. Perhaps he *should* have telephoned Risa. . . . With Donald there it would seem quite

110

natural to contact her, to make plans for a date after the New Year, dinner at maybe that new Italian restaurant in the underground area of the Westgate Mall, afterward a movie.... Unless Cynthia objected. Would she object? Eventually the boys will meet Risa anyway, that certainly can't be avoided, the sane, reasonable thing to do is accept it, as Edwin has explained to her lawyer innumerable times. As Edwin has explained....

Risa's odd behavior. Kittenish and shrewd and unpredictable. Returning from Marrakech with a lovely golden suntan and a tiny red tattoo on her shoulder. A tattoo! And not only denying Edwin's charges (which he could back by evidence, evidence gathered for him by Scott Investigative Services) that she had gone on the trip not solely with a girl friend but in the company of Da Vinci Pollock and another man, not only denying these charges, but lashing out venomously at Edwin himself for doubting her . . . ! She gave him back the ring. He gave it back to *her*. She accepted it under the condition that she needn't wear it until she felt "right" about him again.

Six weeks ago, approximately. Late October. Miserable evenings spent in The Whale's Belly, alone, hurried and tasteless dinners at Tin Roy's and The Red Dragon, flowers sent to her apartment, letters, and even a telegram: I love you I forgive you anything please forgive me please call or allow me to call. Her silence. Sullen stubborn silence. If he telephoned sometimes there was no answer, he stood with the phone in his hand in the half-furnished apartment, in the dark, counting the rings, begging her to answer. Unless she was away. Unless there was another man with her.

Da Vinci Pollock—! She had gone to Marrakech with *him*.
I did nothing of the sort. I won't be spied on, she screamed.
But there is evidence—
I won't be spied on! Get out of here!
You were wearing my ring, I sent you on the trip because

you said you were so exhausted, you couldn't even wait until I could take two weeks off—

That's ridiculous, that's completely ridiculous! Now get out of here, I want to go to bed.

Da Vinci Pollock of all people—

Get out! Get out!

Later it crossed his mind that perhaps she had not been with Pollock, exactly. Perhaps the other girl had been with Pollock.

(Scott Investigative Services sent him a bill for $320. And he had already paid a $100 retaining fee.)

Six weeks of her capricious behavior. Of course she loved him: she never retracted that. And wanted to marry him. And *would* marry him. But the notion struck her, he certainly didn't know why, that she should not wear his ring—a beautiful 24-carat diamond—until he was officially divorced from his wife. I want to feel right about you in every way, she said.

A beribboned pot of white mums, a fresh display of daisies and roses and violets, a box of Fanny Farmer chocolates, an alligator-hide handbag from Woodland Imports: gifts purchased on his credit card and sent into the abyss of her Westgate apartment. At least she did not send them back, Edwin thinks. If she was truly angry with him she would send the presents back.

Love. Desire. His anguish at the thought of her, the realization that *at this very moment* he could be making love to her—a realization that stuns him a dozen times daily. He could be with Risa, lying in her arms, grappling with her, nuzzling her, kissing her, conquering her lively long-legged body with his own. He could be with *her* instead of—instead of where he happens to be.

The time? Moving along. But still a while to go. *Still* a while to go.

Donald is clapping and whistling. Stamping his feet like the others. A good imitation, Edwin thinks. He too should make

112

the effort, he supposes: father attending basketball game with son, caught up in the feverish excitement though of course he doesn't know any of the players and is really thinking of— Actually he is thirsty. How very good a beer would taste, a cold beer. The sudden desire for beer blots out even his troubled amorous thoughts of Risa.

Would it be too obvious, he wonders, if he slips away; hurries to the car and drives to a nearby tavern and has just one beer, or maybe two; and returns within half an hour. Would Donnie even notice, would Donnie care? Would he hold it against him?

No, better not. Maybe after the game. A late snack for Donnie, a beer for himself, excellent idea, father and son, talking over the game. His thirst, though powerful, can wait. Will wait. Perhaps, he thinks suddenly, his heart ballooning, he can treat some of Donald's friends. Round up a half-dozen kids and drive them over to Farmer Si's where they can have hamburgers and french fries and milkshakes, whatever kids their age like, and he can have beer on tap. The kids will really appreciate it, maybe they will invite Donald to their homes, to parties, maybe he will have his first girl friend as a consequence, go on double-dates . . . and even if Cynthia hears about the beer (though who would tell her?—not Donnie) she certainly could not object to Edwin's generosity. You never take time with either of the boys, she used to say. You never. . . .

So he decides not to slip away. Remain right where he is. Hot, uncomfortable, thirsty. Bored. He will force himself to pay closer attention to what is happening on the court—force himself to whistle and applaud like the other fathers, and even to make loud noises of disappointment, whenever appropriate.

Waiting in the corridor, on the stairs. Hundreds of kids passing by. The building fairly trembles with their footsteps.

Donald, his arms folded across his thin chest, leans against the railing, stony-faced, silent. Edwin murmurs: "... can't imagine why in hell you're so set against it, there's no harm in asking.... Those kids will be *delighted,* I remember when I was that.... And the girl especially, what was her name, Fran?—she was very friendly, I got the distinct impression that.... Well, she *likes* you. I remember when I was that age.... But where is she? Where are they? It took us so long to push out here, I *told* you we should have slipped out a side door before the game was over ... a minute or two wouldn't have hurt, would it.... Avoid all this congestion ... so unpleasant.... Something dizzying about a crowd like this.... Do you think she's already gone? Maybe if we hurried out into the parking lot...."

He tries to keep the disappointment out of his voice. Standing on the fifth or sixth step, staring at the milling crowd, the jostling noisy rowdy streams of children, strangers' children, filing out into the cold December night past security guards—standing there he feels a sensation of sudden terrible loss. So many children! So many faces! None of them glances his way, none of them shows the slightest curiosity about him. He stares, invisible, his eyes burning. And there is a ticklish burning sensation in his throat. After some minutes, as the crowd thins, he says to Donald: "Well. She must have left ahead of us."

"It's okay, Dad," Donald replies.

VIII.

The Key

And now here. Look. Friday, January 21, 6:15 P.M. The dim, pinkly-lit Costa del Sol Lounge just off the main entrance of the Conquistador Motor Inn in Bethel Park, a suburb twenty miles north of Woodland. A solitary woman at the bar, in a high-necked but backless dress. A blond woman. Attractive. Smoking a cigarette thoughtfully. Not frowning, not melancholy or troubled; but thoughtful. Mysterious. A woman of substance. Character. Sitting at the nearly deserted bar, pert and straight-backed and somehow provocative on one of the little leather stools, her waist and hips clearly defined in the clinging black silk dress, her naked back defiantly white: a woman Edwin has never set eyes on before, smoking a cigarette languidly and stirring the ice in her drink.

Look. It is happening as he has planned. As he has rehearsed.

He enters the lounge hesitantly, almost timidly, though he knows that his appearance, this evening, is impressive. (A new sports jacket, brown with brass buttons, and new dark trousers; his most attractive necktie, a beige knit; his hair freshly cut and shampooed and blown dry.) A few of the patrons glance around, the bartender gives him an indifferent appraisal, but the woman in the backless dress does not seem to notice.

Edwin wonders—Is she alone at the Motor Inn? Or is she

115

simply awaiting a husband or an escort?—or a lover? Sitting at the bar, waiting for a man. Her lover, perhaps. A woman like that *would* have a lover. Lovers.

He sees with a small thrill of excitement that her left hand is ringless. (Though she is wearing an oversized dinner ring on her right hand, possibly a topaz. Is it in bad taste, or is it merely daring, a reckless flamboyant gesture? It seems quite clear from the way she plays with the swizzle stick in her drink that she is an independent, perhaps even a somewhat spoiled woman.) Unmarried. Solitary. Very attractive—very. And so timidly, and boldly, Edwin Locke approaches the bar. His silly heart is pounding. Veins at his temples are pounding.

The risk of it. Once again. The blind gasping plunge.

Cheerfully he has said to himself, up in the room, dabbing cologne on his throat, his jaw: What can I lose. What can I lose.

Ah, the woman *is* attractive. Heavily but skillfully made up. Sharply-defined lips, very red. Stylish hair, wavy, shaved up the back of her slender throat. Tiny gold earrings, for pierced ears. A somewhat snubbed nose. And that bare, palely-gleaming back, the tiny knuckle-bones of vertebrae, a sight that Edwin finds mesmerizing, as if he has never seen anything quite like it before.

The woman's profile is indifferent, even haughty. She must be aware of Edwin's presence but she does not glance around.

"Are you. . . . May I join. . . ."

He swallows his words miserably. So timid! Such a fool! The woman finally looks around, her lips parting damply, in expectation. Her carefully arched eyebrows register curiosity. A cool, almost contemptuous curiosity. Edwin repeats his question, smiling like a fool, like an adolescent boy, and the woman stares at him in silence. Her eyes are thickly outlined with black pencil, brightly keen. She is young. Well, fairly. A mature woman with a glowing youthful sensuous face. It is

116

obvious from the way she sits at the bar, her breasts pressing against the leather rim, that she is a sensuous, experienced woman, a woman of mysterious substance and character. It is obvious that. . . .

Edwin pulls over a bar stool. Sits. Sweating, smiling. He orders a Scotch from the bored bartender, who is dressed in a toreador jacket. He asks the woman if she is alone. Or waiting for someone. Alone? Yes. Alone. Asks her what she is drinking. And would she like another. Yes? . . . The lounge is quite attractive, isn't it. The black leather. The red and pink lampshades. The bullfighting motif in a bronze bas-relief above the bar. The Conquistador itself is quite attractive, one of the newer motels in this area. The restaurant, they say, is quite adequate. Over-priced (but aren't they all) but adequate.

The woman nods but her manner is still somewhat haughty, withdrawn. Edwin tries to think of something to say, to ask. He *could* inquire about her background: is she married, has she ever been married, has she any children, has she been, well, *wounded* by life, as he has. But she is so coolly remote, so tantalizingly distant. Ah, she knows him!—she knows how to tease! He hears himself saying something about the weather. Ever since early December it's been so grim and cheerless, hasn't it. And that blizzard on New Year's Day. Funny, as you get older time is supposed to go more rapidly, and in many ways it *does* (now why in Christ's name am I saying this, Edwin wonders in dismay, but cannot stop, and cannot change the subject), but that isn't true of the winter, is it. In fact the winter seems to hang on forever.

"Yes. I suppose so," the woman says neutrally.

He has an urge to seize her small pert defiant chin and turn her face to him. What then! What then?

In a corner of the lounge a solitary patron is playing an electronic game, muttering and chuckling to himself with drunken innocence. The bartender, wiping glasses, yawns

117

loudly. (Edwin must suppress a nervous reflex—seeing another person yawn he quite naturally wants to yawn, himself. Odd, odd. Or is that reflex fairly normal?)

What to say? What to say? He tries to remember what he has rehearsed. In his imagination the woman was far more acquiescent, her face was turned fully toward him, her lips and eyes melting. . . . He fumbles in his pocket for cigarettes. But with an exquisitely casual gesture the woman pushes *her* pack toward him. . . .

"Hey. Thanks. That's very sweet," he whispers.

The woman's smile is wry and knowing. She is not young, nor is she pretty any longer, despite her clever make-up; but Edwin feels almost faint with excitement and apprehension. He leans toward her, smiling. He inhales her perfume with gratitude. Something musky, something very provocative. And the look of her naked back, the tiny bones appearing to shiver slightly beneath the fine pale envelope of skin. . . .

"You're very. . . . You're. . . ."

He swallows suddenly. Has to fight an impulse to cough.

". . . a very attractive woman. *Very* attractive."

Her nostrils widen as she draws in her breath, considering his remark. Then she says with admirable evenness: "You're a very attractive man."

Edwin sips at his drink. Says quickly: "As soon as I came in the doorway I noticed you. And wanted you. I mean that—just the way it sounds. I saw you sitting here and I wanted you, just like that. I'm the kind of man who . . . who. . . . I'm the kind of man who knows what he likes, in a woman. Who is able to appreciate . . . who is able to appreciate a womanly woman. A woman who knows . . . who knows about certain things. Who isn't coy. Who isn't self-conscious. As soon as I came in the doorway and saw you here I *knew*."

The woman laughs lightly, but Edwin can see that he has startled her. "Is that so," she drawls.

118

"I imagine you know what you want too. In a man. I imagine you aren't shy about ... about expressing yourself," Edwin says softly.

Half-closes his eyes. Waits. What will happen next, what *should* happen next ... ? He is quite excited. The woman too is, or should be, excited. Sexual tension: unmistakable. The way she is sitting ... the way she avoids his eye. She *should* be excited. Is. Is excited. Must try to imagine the sensations arising in her, in the pit of her belly, between her thighs, would it be an ache, would it be a nervous tingling feeling, a sense of ... of yearning ... ? Yearning to be filled? Completed? By him? By *him?*

He lights a cigarette. Bloody damn nuisance: has to flick the lighter several times before a flame catches. One two three four *five....*

She lifts her glass. Drains it in one long swallow.

"... a woman like you, with a ... a body like yours.... A mature, sensuous, *knowing....*"

"Mature?"

"... experienced. Widely and, and variedly ... and knowledgeably experienced."

The woman considers his words, staring at the glass in her hand. Edwin sees, and appreciates, that her fingernails have been painted a dramatic golden-bronze. How odd, how beguiling, a color! He doesn't think he has ever seen it before, close up, on a real woman, a *real* person. "And you," she whispers, "what about you?"

"Me? Oh. Well. *Me,*" Edwin says, going blank for a moment. "I am ... I am the kind of man.... I am the kind of man, honey, who knows what he likes, in a woman. I mean I can appreciate.... I can *see....* Well, there are things that another man might not notice, but ... I have had some interesting experiences with women. Some very, very interesting experiences."

119

"Have you," she says, a trifle sharply. And then, in a more subdued throaty voice: "Oh. *Have* you."

"And the one thing I learned, the one thing I absolutely learned, was ... was.... The one thing I am in fact *still* learning ... is that a woman's sensuality is far deeper and more complex and ... and astonishing ... and even alarming ... than a man's. This is something all men should—"

"Alarming, why? Did you say alarming?"

"Astonishing. Amazing. Just fantastic," Edwin says, shaking his head. "I mean *fantastic*.... *You* know what I mean."

The woman giggles suddenly. "I'm not sure if I do."

"Yes, you do. *You* know."

"Do I?"

"With a, a body like yours.... Those hips and ... and breasts.... Your mouth.... Oh you know, you know," he says, giggling himself, trying hard to resist a sudden spasm of coughing. "I mean it stands out. It announces itself. Why, as soon as I came in the door, the doorway, as soon as my gaze fastened on.... Well I mean I knew. I just knew. And," he says, lowering his voice, trembling, "I wanted you. In that instant."

"Did you. Did you really," the woman says.

"Obviously. Can't you tell."

"... another drink?"

"What? Yes?"

"Are we going to have another drink?"

"Yes. Certainly.... What time is it?"

"Early."

"Early. Yes. Fine. Another drink. Two more, in fact. ... And then, do you think we might, do you think you'd enjoy ... well, coming upstairs with me...."

"To your room?"

"To my room. Where we can continue our discussion in absolute privacy."

120

"But we hardly know each other. I don't even know your name."

"Is that important? Are names so important to you?"

She smirks. No, it is a smile, a frightened little smile.

"No. Of course not. You should be able to tell that, just by looking at me," she says slowly, vaguely.

"The room is a very attractive one. In fact it's a suite. A honeymoon suite, I believe. . . . At a special discount."

"What sort of discount?"

". . . a sunken bathtub, of marble . . . an enormous heart-shaped bed . . . a dozen pillows . . . a thick plush rug . . . lamps with shades of pink and scarlet . . . flowers, fresh flowers . . . and candles . . . and incense. . . . And on closed-circuit television, if we should want it, certain films, certain frankly *erotic* films . . . as the advertising brochure says. But I don't really think, do you, that we will need such things," Edwin says breathlessly.

"Is there music? There must be music," the woman says, blushing faintly.

"I think so. Yes. Piped-in. Throbbing and sensual. Spanish, I think. Spanish flamenco. I think."

"But we don't know each other. We don't know each other's *name.*"

Edwin laughs, raising his glass in a toast. His laughter becomes wheezing but he manages to get it under control. ". . . name? Why? Such an outmoded convention. . . . And you don't look at all like a conventional woman."

"Maybe I'm not. But still."

". . . beneath your clothes, for instance."

"Beneath what? Why?"

"In your flesh. In your skin. *There* you aren't a conventional woman, are you. But all women. Sharing in their secrets. . . ."

She giggles suddenly. Finishes her drink.

"And now," Edwin says, grinning. "Now. I think it's about

121

time, don't you."

"Well—"

"I *think* it's about time we adjourned to room 255."

"Do you have the key?"

"Of course," Edwin says, patting his pocket. The key is attached to an oversized Spanish "coin" of plastic; he slipped it into his pocket on the way down, having left the lights in the room turned low and the Muzak dial on *background*. But though his fingers fully expect to touch the key they come away baffled. "That is I *think*...."

The woman snatches up her purse. Opens it. Takes out a compact. Dabs at her nose with a powder puff, rather impatiently. "Have you lost the key?" she asks.

"It's here somewhere. It must be," Edwin mutters. He searches the pockets of his sports coat. Odd. Very odd. He tries his trouser pockets. No? But where ... ? Avoiding the woman's gaze he tries all his pockets again. *Is* it lost? Did someone pick his pocket on the way down? Or ...? "Oh Christ," he says, "I put it in my other coat. I was going to wear my other coat. ... Not that it matters, of course. I can pick another key up at the front desk."

The woman closes her purse with an angry snap. Edwin sees, surprised, that her expression is stiff with bemused contempt. "Can you," she whispers. "Can you really."

"What do you mean? I don't ... I don't understand...."

"Tonight of all nights. Deliberately. And you're drunk, aren't you. You were drinking before you met me. And you saw to it that I'm drunk. Didn't you. And that tie—the dry cleaners never got that gravy stain out of it, can't you see?—can't you for God's sake *see!* I thought I'd thrown that thing out years ago but somehow you still *have* it, you must have *hoarded* it...." She begins to cry, her shoulders shaking, her face distorted. "Tonight of all nights. Oh Edwin, *tonight of all nights.*"

"But—but— But I can pick up another key at the front desk, can't I?" Edwin asks, astonished.

IX.

Love Therapy

Edwin Locke, a little less than nine months before his death, stares, at first uncomprehending (he has been at The Round Table, at a rather lengthy business luncheon, and he feels somewhat shaky on his feet) at the pink telephone messages his secretary has given him. Three from *Mrs. Locke.* Please call back as soon as possible. Urgent. 11:50 A.M. And another at 2:15 P.M. And another at 3. But who is *Mrs. Locke?* Who is she to make demands upon him?

There are messages from his attorney Joe Bushy, and Cynthia's attorney Fred Bagot; these calls he supposes he must return, eventually. But as for Cynthia's emotional blackmail—and after their agreement in January!—after their disastrous attempt at a reconciliation, and their subsequent agreement to let each other alone!—before his secretary has time even to leave his office, he mutters loudly, "No you don't, you bitch," and tears the slips into several pieces and drops them into his handsome leather wastebasket.

Edna-Mae Brewer giggles, startled.

For a moment neither speaks. Edwin feels short of breath, his heart pumping with righteous anger. The bitch! Blackmailing him! After the ugly unforgivable things she said! After their vows not to harass each other, but to communicate through their lawyers!

He sways, staring into his wastebasket. Indiscreet, to have

125

torn the slips while little Edna-Mae was observing him. Now she will tell the office. The other girls. And he had not meant—or *had* he—to make her laugh that coy guilty shocked giggle.

He looks at her. Is reassured by her sobriety. A pretty girl, with a curly touselled hair-do like Risa's, but without Risa's superb breasts and hips. And stance. Still, she *is* charming. Not terribly bright but charming. He trusts her. He is very fond of her. Surely she must know, and will not laugh at him. If he could explain the unhappy circumstances of his life....

Rather gravely she says, "But Mr. Locke, it's getting so difficult. What do you want me to tell her? She's even beginning to—well, to accuse me of not giving you her messages."

"She's a sick woman, Edna-Mae. She isn't responsible for what she says."

"Oh— Oh that's—"

"Don't take any abuse from her. Simply be courteous, and firm, and tell her to contact me through Bushy or Bagot."

"Yes. Bushy or Bagot."

"Or Gidding. Yes, tell her Gidding as well," Edwin says.

"Bushy or Bagot or Gidding."

As she backs away, smiling with gentle sad sympathy, flicking a curly strand of red-brown hair off her forehead, she murmurs, "I'm just so sorry to hear... I mean about Mrs. Locke.... If there's ever anything I can do.... I mean.... She sounds so sort of *furious* on the phone and I... I feel sorry for you.... And.... Well, anyway, I just wanted you to know."

"You're very sweet, Edna-Mae," Edwin says with sudden warmth.

She laughs again, as though surprised. But not terribly surprised.

"Why thank you, Mr. Locke, that's sweet of *you* to say."

Attempted reconciliation. Tears and long draining hours of

talk and "forgiveness" (on Cynthia's part—bequeathed as though she were handing out alms to beggars, or curing scrofula with a touch of her hand) and the determination, feverish, even grim, to save their marriage.

Sometimes things are strongest where they are broken.

Aren't they?

... *save* the marriage, *cement* it together, begin again with a new, a firm, a stronger foundation. So they decided, that freezing New Year's Day when, after having lived through the most horror-filled night of his life (the panic of utter aloneness; the panic of his knowledge that he was about to slip into insanity; the heart-sickening gut-sickening panic of his realization that Risa would never, never marry him; and would not, in fact, even see him again) he returned home, to Cynthia and the boys, begging forgiveness, begging their understanding.

Please. Please. Please. Don't reject me.

Oh please love me.

I am so sad, so very sad, I am so lonely and sad and. . . .

Of Risa, not a word. And why should he speak of her, to his good-hearted warm-hearted wife. A bitch, wasn't she, an opportunist, a tramp, a whore. Certainly—a whore! Who took him for thousands of dollars. Yes indeed. Thousands. Thousands of dollars. But Cynthia, cradling his head against her breasts, not minding if the front of her dress dampened from his tears, need not know about *that;* it would complicate matters unnecessarily.

He talked and talked and talked. Hugged her. Pressed his face against her neck, her breasts, her belly. Spoke of his loneliness. His habit of drinking too much. Talking to himself, calling himself names, half-willing an accident on the expressway, half-willing sickness. Could she ever forgive him? Could she ever take him back?

(The boys were downstairs, hushed. Waiting. When he'd come in the house Teddy had run to him at once—Teddy, whom he thought he had lost—and hugged him, and they wept together; and though Donald was more cautious, more restrained, he too eventually came to his father and allowed himself to be hugged. Edwin saw, and was deeply moved by, a glint of tears in Donald's eyes.)

Reconciliation. But a rational, intelligent, *conscious* reconciliation. So Cynthia insisted, and Edwin agreed. They would make an appointment as soon as possible with a marriage therapist. Cynthia had heard by way of Gina by way of Florence that the Diehls had had marital difficulties last fall and had gone to a therapist by the name of Gidding who had an office, Cynthia believed, right in Woodland; in fact, in the new Maddox Building, with the in-door parking and that new restaurant The Buccaneer that everyone seems to like.

Gidding. Dr. Gidding.

Male or female?—Cynthia didn't know. But surely it would not matter, she said, a trifle petulantly, if Dr. Gidding was a woman—would it?

Certainly not. No.

Though if he felt hesitant about discussing frank matters, frank personal intimate matters, with a woman—

Of course not, Edwin said.

And so: New Year's Day. A very long tumultuous day. A turning-point in all their lives. Edwin and Cynthia and Donald and Teddy. But after a late supper, when Edwin rose to leave, to return to his apartment in the Place Rivière, both the boys looked alarmed. But isn't Daddy—? Isn't Daddy going to stay here—?

Not tonight, Edwin said bravely. Your mother and I think it might be premature. We are going to work things out like two intelligent, civilized human beings; we are going to admit our limitations and get some professional help. Because, you see, Daddy isn't ready. I mean Daddy isn't worthy.

We think it best, Cynthia said, dabbing at her reddened nose

128

with a tissue, if we work in stages. So Daddy won't be moving back home right away. But he'll see us more often.

God yes. Oh God, yes, Edwin whispered.

Afterward, stopping for a quick drink at The Ram's Horn—a pleasant surprise to discover it open, when nearly every other place was closed—Edwin felt oddly, wonderfully, inexplicably *pure*. Like a man convalescing from a serious illness. He was shaky and weak yet somehow chaste; even, in a way difficult to comprehend, *sacred*.

Purged. Yes, that was it: purged.

Do you know, he said to the bartender, I feel *purged*, I feel new as the New Year.

Yes? said the bartender absently. He was wiping the bar with a damp rag, in quick and ever-decreasing circles.

I feel as if—as if I could go around blessing people, Edwin said, tears in his eyes frankly and unashamedly. I feel as if— well—anyway, Happy New Year to you!

Is it, said the bartender.

There is no such thing as normal or perverse, there is only what gives pleasure; what is good and gives pleasure. What makes people *happy*. Do you see? Dr. Gidding asked.

No. Yes.

We must say to ourselves—This is good! This is very good! *This* too is good! We must put aside all, all confining and in-hibiting prejudices and concentrate on what gives pleasure to us and to our partner.

Yes. I see.

Dr. Gidding: short, slight-bodied, with thin red hair that rose from a low, furrowed forehead like a bird's crest. Hint of a moustache. Crinkly red hairs in ears. Tiny pot belly. Nicotine-stained fingers. Squarish blunt not-very-clean nails. A fey smile. A knowing smile. Elfin. A voice surprisingly full and rich, issuing from that small child-like mouth: You see, it is deadly for us to be trapped in stultifying roles. Who is active, and who is passive—that sort of thing. Who is dominant and who is submissive; who is to blame, who is guiltless. Even the roles of husband and wife! And of course father and mother. The masculine, the feminine. All roles. Games. Habits. Do you see, Edwin?

I see. Yes. I think I see.

Over the years you and your wife have become trapped in your respective roles. And now, in recent months, you have quite inadvertently trapped yourself once again—you are the unfaithful husband, she is the betrayed wife.

Ah yes. Yes.

You are guilty. She guiltless. And so—perhaps—you resent her. Even more than she resents you.

I don't *think* so, Edwin said hesitantly.

But you are the very picture of a guilty man! Dr. Gidding said expansively. And laughed, laughed.

Well I suppose I do feel—I do feel ashamed. As if I'd wronged her. And of course the boys. But I want to make it up to her and I *will.*

Certainly you will, Dr. Gidding said.

Dr. Gidding's office high in the Maddox Building. Not a very large office but a handsome one. A single receptionist, an attractive mature woman with glasses. Bright welcoming smile to Edwin and Cynthia when they came together, the first time. Hello! You must be the Lockes?

$75 an hour. Seems rather high. No: probably quite reasonable, these days.

Why am I thinking of squid, Edwin wondered, waiting in the outer office while Dr. Gidding talked with Cynthia. ... He leafed through copies of Psychology Today, Sailing, The New Yorker. Tried not to think of what she might be telling the therapist.

130

This will take courage, Cynthia murmured in the elevator. Her dark suede coat with the muskrat collar; smart leather boots; self-conscious posture. He squeezed her fingers and smiled. He was the husband, she the wife.

A panic thought: that he might ask the receptionist if he could use the office phone, that he might find himself dialling Risa's number.

And then what! And then what!

Cynthia returned, her eyes reddened, cheeks damp. Dr. Gidding accompanied her to the door. I think I will take a taxi home, she said, gazing at Edwin. (A look he could not decipher. Anguish? Love? Awe? Pain? Bewilderment?)

Yes, my dear. My love.

My sweet wronged wife.

In Dr. Gidding's inner office, facing Dr. Gidding across a glass-topped desk comfortably cluttered with notebooks, sheets of paper, envelopes, well-sharpened pencils. No couch to lie on, at least, Edwin thought with relief. He squinted at the therapist's small furrowed brightly-clever face and drew a deep breath. He would tell no lies: would answer all questions, no matter how humiliating.

Talk to me, Dr. Gidding said in a frank, simple manner. Just talk to me.

About—?

About your marriage. Your life. Your dreams.

I—

Yes?

(I am thinking of squid, Edwin wanted to say, suddenly, horribly. But why in Christ's name am I thinking of squid!)

I am basically a very . . . a very conventional person.

Ah!

And I love my wife, and my boys. And I like my job. I mean I find it challenging. I am content with my home, my friends, my neighborhood, my country. I mean I really *am* content

131

with them. I know I have every reason to be grateful.

But you're not?

Not? What?

Grateful?

Oh yes, yes I am. I'm immensely grateful. If I was a religious man—which I'm not—I guess I'd be down on my knees half the time, just thanking God for what I have. But you know how it is! Edwin said with a sigh, and a melancholy laugh. We always take things for granted.

Your wife tells me, Dr. Gidding said softly, that you have problems.

Problems?

Haven't you?—haven't you problems?

You mean my leaving home and getting mixed up with—

No, no. That was just the consequence.

I don't understand, Edwin said blankly.

The consequence of your deep-seated problems.

What problems?

Don't you know of any? In your relationship with your wife?

In what—in what sense?

Your sexual relationship?

Edwin stares at Dr. Gidding's squarish nails, which were a queer dull plum color.

Oh you bitch, Cynthia!

Aloud he said: My wife has always exaggerated things.

Is that so?

She takes everything so personally....

Silence. Dr. Gidding sat absolutely immobile, watching him with a half-amused half-sympathetic smile. Finally Edwin said: It's true that .. from time to time ... I have had ... I have had difficulty.... I have had some difficulty ... in....

You have experienced impotence? Dr. Gidding asked.

132

I had never... thought of it that way, Edwin said. I....
I....

How did you think of it, then?

I thought of it as ... as ... I'm often so fatigued, he said,
half-sobbing. I mean with my job. The trips to New York, the
hours at the office, the expressway.... I am so fatigued, sometimes I want to die.

Just talk to me, Edwin. Talk.

But there's nothing to talk about!

Your wife, your marriage, your—

It isn't a problem of *mine*. It's just something that happens.
Sometimes. With her. I mean with her and me. I can be ready
to make love with my wife and then... and then my mind
slips away... and I forget where I am. Or something distracts
me: an airplane overhead, a lawnmower outside, the recollec-
tion of something I have to do. It isn't my fault. I can't really
see it as my fault.

In such matters, Dr. Gidding said in a low, soothing voice,
there is no "fault." No one is to blame, and no one is innocent.

It's always something out there, Edwin said hotly. I
mean—it isn't something in me.

Ah but Edwin, in matters of sexual love there is no "out
there," all reality is interior. The principal sexual organ is the
brain.

The brain!

The brain.

Afterward the smiling receptionist asked how he would like
to pay—after each session, or should the office bill him at the
end of the month?

The blond woman at the bar, in the backless silk dress.
Lush-bodied. Sensuous. Languidly smoking a cigarette.
Alone? No lover? No husband?

Golden-bronze fingernails.

133

Full snug breasts.

In matters of sexual love there is no shame, no blame, Dr. Gidding taught. So Edwin whispered, pulling a bar stool over.... May I buy you a drink? You *are* alone?

Cynthia's brave strained face. A slightly feverish look, a brief glare of mockery, abandon. Pushing her package of cigarettes toward him. What sort of discount on the room? Well, this is the off-season. Everyone goes to Florida, or Palm Springs, or the islands. And couples who are having affairs (so it's said) never choose the weekends because they have to be with their families on the weekends. So we're being given a 10% discount.

At these prices, Cynthia said, that isn't much of a bargain.

I suppose not. No.

Still.

The Honeymoon Suite. Immense heart-shaped bed with a scarlet bedspread and dozens of little pillows, covered in satin and wool. A sunken bathtub, of simulated marble. Bath oils, bubble-bath. Big pink creamy bars of soap. Many mirrors. Oh yes: mirrors. Floor-to-ceiling mirrors.

Music: *The Bolero* performed by a Moog synthesizer, heavily but eerily erotic, coiling upward, onward, with terrible unstoppable force. And fresh-cut flowers in an ebony vase in the shape of a woman's body. And thick squat suggestively-shaped candles to be lit, and incense to be burned, and jars of perfumed oils and ointments and lotions. No talk of problems, in fact no talk at all is preferred, Dr. Gidding's wise voice pursued them, you are strangers meeting for the first time, you are coming together in a spontaneous and archetypal union exclusive of role-playing, past and future, outdated notions of guilt and sin and shame and modesty. Say to yourself *Yes— this is good! This is good! Whatever gives pleasure to my partner and me is good, good!*

In the mirrors semi-refracted nude figures leapt antically

134

from frame to frame. Males, females. Hesitant. Stumbling. There were a half-dozen of them and then a dozen, and then more, a small army of men and women wearing their nudity like slightly rumpled, sagging clothes. I love you, I desire you, your body is beautiful, each part of your body is beautiful, Edwin chanted, the echo of Dr. Gidding's voice close behind his. The blond woman was no longer in the backless silk dress. Her hair was now somewhat dishevelled. You are a very, very attractive woman, Edwin whispered, as she whispered, stroking him methodically, you are a very, very attractive man. Stroking, kissing, even hand-holding at this point. A process not to be hurried. No pressure, no sense of obligation. Admire. Behold and admire each other's beauty.

Then the sacred ritual of oiling. Magic potions, tawny musky odors, *The Bolero* winding higher and higher, with an urgency Edwin had never heard in it before. In sexual love, Dr. Gidding taught on the fourth or fifth visit, there is no past or future: there is only the present moment. Paradise is here, now. Here and now. Consequently the lover *never* thinks of anything beyond his beloved's body and his or her sensuous delight. Anointing, oiling, gently massaging the flesh of the other is a holy rite not to be hurried. If you think of external matters the magic is blighted and so all such thinking is forbidden during Love Therapy.

Squid, Edwin thought.

No: your body is beautiful, you are beautiful, I am in awe of your womanliness, I desire you, I *want* you.

You are a very handsome man. Your chest and your chesthair and ... and....

Your breasts....

The muscles of your thighs....

Dim flickering candlelight, a blessing. Even the incense smoke, though it smells like burnt toast or a scorched cooking pan, is a blessing. Love play. Stroking and admiring and kiss-

135

ing and sucking, gently. Gently. No hurry. (The reservation for dinner in The Matador Steak House adjacent to the motel is for 9 P.M. and since it is now 7:25 there is no need to hurry.) This soft fuzz, this frizzy funny ticklish hair. . . . This patch of freckles. . . . (Your thigh muscles: how is it possible they're so hard, you don't *do* anything, is it all from handball once a week?) In matters of sexual love there is no anagogic or abstract experience, Dr. Gidding lectured, no digital information, everything is immediate, holistic, concrete, experiential, existential. It cannot be translated into anything else, it cannot be paraphrased, do you understand? Edwin murmured yes, he thought so, yes he did understand, yet it was quite a revelation.

The blond woman, her body oiled and perfumed and eager, expectant, tensed with an urgency reflected by, or perhaps stimulated by, the rising yearning music. The blond woman with the queer rather silly rather sad golden fingernails. Tiny goose-bumps circling her nipples. (Was one breast scarred? No. Thank God, no.) A muffled belch, a slight odor of gin. A rumbling stomach. (His own, Edwin thought with some chagrin. Or was it hers? . . . He had not eaten much at noon, having been apprehensive about tonight.) Incense, flickering shadows, thank God the naked men and women were no longer visible in the mirrors, thank God they were lying out of sight, discreetly out of sight, on the heart-shaped bed.

In matters of sexual love, Dr. Gidding's voice floated near, a little more sharply Dr. Gidding's voice penetrated the delirious heaving music, there is no right or wrong or normal or perverse or good or bad or nice or wicked or superior or inferior, in matters of sexual love there is only immediate sensuous reality, the mystic Now, the Eternal Yea-Saying Present, do you understand? No, Edwin whimpered, yes, I understand, yes, eagerly kissing the blond woman's thighs, and the insides of her thighs, his eyes shut tight. Yes. I understand.

136

$75 an hour. A bill at the end of the month.

Ah but wait: $75 an hour *for each of them.*

Do you think we should report Gidding to the Better Business Bureau, Edwin wants to ask his wife, but Gidding says sharply, No thoughts! No interfering distracting thoughts! Though it might be rather embarrassing since Larry Hanover is the Bureau's counsel and.... If word got around....

A pulse throbbing in his head. But not yet, not quite yet, in his penis.

Yes—this is good! This is good! And this too! Whatever gives pleasure to my partner and me is—

(7:26, 7:27. Edwin's wristwatch, the numerals glowing slowly in the semi-dark. Slyly and rather mockingly.)

(Dinner—not until 9 P.M.)

In matters of sexual love there must be no inhibitions, no holding-back of desire, Dr. Gidding's voice insisted, floating near. Edwin, gripping his partner's plump, rather soft, rather raddled buttocks, feels a sudden pang of utter loneliness. Dr. Gidding, I am going to cry, he thinks, oh Dr. Gidding, I am going to burst into tears. I am so lonely. I am so lonely.

Flesh that must be performed in terms of another's flesh.

So lonely.

Daddy is not ready yet. I mean not worthy.

Panting. Moaning. Urgency. Anticipation. Step by step the love-process progresses, without hurry, without any sense of *obligation.* This, of course, is highly important. If the male should feel some difficulty in becoming properly aroused....

A woman's hands feverishly stroking. Anointed perfumed flesh, rather greasy. Lardish-tasting.

Thousands of dollars. The muddy parking lot of The Way. Bill from the dentist, Risa's friend. (So high! For that simple dental work! *Did Risa get a kick-back from the little Paki bastard?*)

I love you, Edwin, the woman is whispering, moaning, I

love you, I *want* you, for the first time in my life I know what love is and I know what desire is. But why, Edwin thinks miserably, don't the Diehls move to Boston, has Charles's offer been withdrawn . . . ?

In matters of sexual love, Dr. Gidding urges, it is imperative that you never forget that—

A bride of one day. Old inn. Maine. Stormy overcast Atlantic skies. Do you love me, my God of course I love you, I am so happy I think I will burst into tears. The Volkswagen stalling at the foot of a hill! Oh God damn it, wouldn't you know it. . . . For the past year you've been acting half-insane. You simply haven't been normal. You drink too much, you're absent-minded around the house, you don't hear half of what I tell you, you neglect the boys. I can't live like this.

Querulous questioning stomach-murmur. What time is it? Oh God only 7:31.

I am so lonely. When I dialled that bitch's number my hand shook and I got the wrong party, a black woman answered, sounded angry and disappointed. Sorry sorry sorry sorry. They want to bury me along with him, I am not ready, Daddy isn't ready. Wait. Oh you bitch, I'll show you! Da Vinci blacking your eye will be nothing compared to what I will do.

Straddling her hot naked struggling body. The chin gripped firmly, hair streaming out in terror. Or: slapping her face, one cheek and then the other, slowly, methodically. Take that. And that. And that. And that.

If the male continues to experience difficulty in. . . .

Shut up! Don't lie to me! You slut, you shameless whore!

The erotic films? But no. Too late. Embarrassed to bring the subject up anyway. That magazine on my desk, was it Monday, and Edna-Mae carried off the Sinclair portfolio, and. . . . A moment of exquisite embarrassment. Oh my God yes.

Edna-Mae?

Grimly he summons faces. A small familiar procession of

138

faces. Babs McIntire from math class, tenth grade was it, oh yes and that girl with the knee sox DeeDee Duncan, and... and Cathleen Diehl... no, not Cathleen... the waitress at the Tip-Top... no, too much like Risa... well, Risa herself in the leather boots, the lynx coat, sunglasses... but the dog is barking... lunging at his ankles.... Cynthia downstairs in the lounge: her naked shimmering back, her averted face, solitary stranger, mysterious, unfathomable, lewd. But. No. Babs McIntire. The girl with the pixie cut, chewing gum, all that mascara, in the coffee shop downstairs; evidently works at Bank of America in the Mall. A knowing blurry somewhat smeared, smutty smile one day. No? Yes? Fran. Little Fran. Poking Donnie with her elbow. Soiled, sly, lascivious, leering. At that age! No more than fourteen! Still: DeeDee Duncan, the rumors about her, how Jeff Hollander bragged, boasted, the back seat of his older brother's car, and DeeDee was only fifteen, no more than fifteen. Risa. Dancing with Da Vinci Pollock. (Do they dance? Or are the dances now wild discotheque things, men and woman gyrating without coming into contact?) Pollock blacking her eye. Slapping one cheek, then the other. Take this, you bitch! Slut! Whore! Filthy tramp!... Edna-Mae. Fran. Cathleen. Squid.

He laughs suddenly.

Laughs. Wheezing and snorting.

What's wrong, Cynthia cries, but he cannot stop laughing. Face, lips, even his tongue, oily, tasting of grease, perfume. Cannot stop laughing. Cannot. What's wrong, why are you laughing, stop, stop it, have you gone crazy?

Gasping, snorting. Tears spilling from his shut eyes.

Stop it! You bastard!

Cannot.

Oh I hate you, I hate you! —Suddenly kicking at him, slapping at him. Her nails scraping his wet chest. He begins to cough uncontrollably. A sudden pain in his jaw, where one of her long nails catches him. Oh I hate you, you'll pay for this, you will never see the boys again, I'll have you arrested if you set foot on my property again, you son of a bitch, you ignorant ugly lying alcoholic son of a bitch, I only married you because my cousin Janet was getting married, I don't think I ever really loved you, I just talked myself into doing it, I was so stupid I would have married anyone who came along—

Edwin rolls onto the floor, half-sobbing, his oily body picking up lint and dust from the carpet. Oh I hate you, oh you bastard, you lying alcoholic bastard, Cynthia screams at him, on her hands and knees now, breasts shaking with rage. It was because of Janet! My entire adult life has been her fault! She was getting married and so *I* had to get married, like a fool, and now I'm forty-three years old and it's too late—

He is convulsed with laughter. Or is it a spasm of sobbing. To protect himself from the hideous woman atop the bed he rolls onto his belly and shields the back of his head with his hands. Don't hit me! Don't hurt me! Oh stop! Help! His naked buttocks quiver. His spine bends, humbling itself. But Cynthia, still screaming at him, shows no mercy: without quite knowing what she does she grabs one of the lighted candles, a thick, squat mustard-colored thing, and throws it at poor Edwin. It strikes him, flame and all, on the small of his back.

Oh don't! Cynthia! Please!

The candle ricochets to the carpet. The flame is snuffed out.

"Mr. Locke? Mr. Locke?"

He wakes. Raises his head from the desk, from his cradling arms.

"Yes? What? What?"

Edna-Mae, smiling apologetically.

Must have fallen asleep.

"I just wondered, Mr. Locke, if.... Well, if you realized what time it is."

140

"Yes. Thanks. Thanks," he says, rubbing his eyes, rubbing his hands through his hair.

Must have fallen asleep for a minute or two.

And then, catching Edna-Mae just as she is slipping into her trim little corduroy coat with the fluffy fur collar (rabbit fur? imitation fur?): "Would you like to stop somewhere for a drink? There's the Gunga-Din on Postman—or maybe the C.O.D. on Fenkell—"

Blinking, moist-lipped, she makes a surprised regretful moue. "Oh I'm sorry, Mr. Locke, but I have to meet my fiancé."

"Oh. Yes. Well."

". . . But, well. Maybe I could, for a while. I mean, I don't have to meet him until 7."

X.

Rub

"You can love your children as much as yourself," Edwin says in a calm passionate voice, "you can love your children *more* than yourself, but that doesn't mean you can get through to them. I mean—how the hell can you get through to someone who just deliberately shuts you out? *Getting through* to my family.... Sometimes the effort makes me so tired.... You know what I mean, don't you?"

The girl does not reply but he notes, with a stab of pleasure, that she appears to have nodded slightly.

Yes?

"... the communication wires, whatever you call it, the very *basis* of ... of communicating ... are down. Fucked-up. (If you'll excuse my language. But I've learned in the past few months to be *frank*. Unless you speak *frankly* nobody comprehends.) Right? Yes? I was reading an article the other day. The media. The electronic media. There's too much information being beamed out and people are talking different languages without knowing it and the worst ... the worst fuck-up is between parents and children because ... did you read this? ... it was in the weekend magazine ... because people like myself are linear and print-oriented and time-conditioned and ... there's something about information systems ... circuits getting overloaded, that kind of thing. The clock, you know. That was given as an example. Not of the

143

electronic media but of ... of something else. For instance, when it was first discovered. Invented. Before that they had what-do-you-call them. ... Things in gardens. You know. A thing in a garden or a park, it's made of metal, it has a pedestal and it's made of concrete and metal and it looks like a sail or a shark's fin ... it throws a shadow. ... I mean if there's sun. If it's during the day. It throws a shadow and you tell time by it. ... That was how they *did* tell time, they didn't have watches. So. What happened was, the clock was invented, and for the first time in history people could ask one another *What time is it?* That was given as ... as an example. Of how things change. I mean, humankind was one way before that question got asked; then it became another way. The point is. ... The point is that the change is irreversible. *What time is it?* The first time in history that anybody—"

The girl has murmured something that sounds like *7:15.* Edwin blinks, somewhat hurt that she has misunderstood, but he does not want to correct her.

"Well. Anyway. The point of the article was, and I agree completely, there are two cultures and they're at war and civilization itself is in danger. Kids watch too much television, they expect easy answers in life, black-and-white statements from their parents, complex situations simplified, a solution for every ... for every tragic crisis. But they can't get them. I mean, a responsible parent doesn't give them those easy answers. For instance, now, if one parent ... for instance the mother, the mother is always *closest* to the children ... if that parent deliberately attempts to poison the children against their father ... painting him as evil, and selfish, and cruel, and some kind of a monster ... just because he has made a decision for freedom, a decision to break out of a suffocating marriage before it's too late ... a decision not to play the game any longer ... the goddam heartbreaking game. ... Well, she's got the advantage. Doesn't she. I mean she's being

144

given possession of the house and the kids are right *there* and the father's visiting rights are an insult, he has to be on his good behavior like it was Sunday School, he has to beg, he's made to feel like a... like a criminal, a leper.... Oh well, Christ. You don't want to hear all this, do you.... Teddy is turning into a brat, and Donald is barely civil, and I get the impression they're just waiting for the visit to end, and the harder I try the more awkward it seems and they don't help me, you know, they don't *help* me at all, I can practically hear their mother's hysterical voice in the air between us, *Don't listen to your father, he's a bad man! He's a bad, bad man! Don't listen to him and don't even look at him, stare right through him like he isn't even there, like he doesn't even exist....* You know it's March now, March 11, and I haven't seen the littlest boy for three weeks and he won't even talk on the phone and there was some kind of a scare about him coming down with pneumonia ... I didn't even think people got pneumonia any more, did you? ... so ... anyway ... they can use that as an excellent excuse for him not seeing me. And they do, they do, believe me! They do. You don't have any children yourself, I suppose...."

Edwin can't see the girl now, so he doesn't know if she shakes her head yes or no; if she has replied he hasn't heard her.

"Well. It's torture. The whole thing in life about... about sacrificing for other people ... for your children.... That whole thing we were taught, it all seems to collapse: and what are you left with? Two snapshots in a billfold. Sometimes it makes me so tired, so bone-weary...."

He is silent for a while. Eyes shut tight. Perspiration running down his forehead, his sides, even his legs. Trickling. Tickling. The principal sexual organ, Dr. Gidding lectures, is the brain. In sexual matters it is imperative that....

"You know," Edwin says, half-sobbing, "I only want to live.

145

I want to live. I have a right, don't I, to *live.* I don't want to die without . . . without having lived. For most of my life I was playing a game but I didn't quite know it. I didn't grasp it. I was playing the game of Edwin. The game of Edwin. When I was a boy I believed that everybody was exactly who they pretended to be and so I must have been the person I was pretending to be but . . . but it's like being back-stage during a play . . . once you *see* the play from that angle it no longer works. And you can't help what you see. Stage make-up and phony histrionic gestures and blinding lights and people talking too loud. . . . Chalk on the floor to indicate where they should stand. . . . Actors. Costumes. Scripts. But nobody else seems to know, that's the hell of it, they keep on with their lines, oh God year after year, they expect you to do the same and become furious when you refuse. . . . Simply because you've seen through the charade! You've caught on! I told her over the phone, I didn't care if she was taping the conversation or not, I said, let the goddam play continue without me, why do you need me, why in Christ's name do you need *me* on stage with you. . . . I want to live, is that so evil? Is that so crazy? The thing is," Edwin says, short of breath, "I've always been young. I've always been young so I didn't mind waiting. When you're young, you know, you don't *mind.* But now. . . . Now suddenly the terrain has shifted, and . . . and things look different. I can't explain. You wouldn't understand, you're too young yourself, you're probably laughing at me, it's the oldest story in the world and you have every right to laugh at me, I know, I know, but. . . . But listen: it hurts as much as if it's the first time, I mean the first time in history. Do you understand? Do you? Please?"

Eiffel Tower. Odd name for a place ten steps down from the sidewalk. Rood Street, Friday evening, downtown, in the area near the Memorial Coliseum, haven't driven through here in years; seedy, run-down; the advantage of perfect anonymity. *Eiffel Tower Body Rub, Parisian Masseuses, Complete Satisfaction Guaranteed.* A relief that the procedure is so impersonal, almost clinical. Very little to do with sex after all. Imagination, mainly. Still it's embarrassing.

Humbling.

What is your name, Edwin asked the girl.

We don't talk to customers, she said in a flat bored voice.

Pasty skin, close-set dark eyes, stringy brown hair, lifeless, a consequence perhaps of the "Roman bath," the steam and heat and airlessness. How old was she, nineteen? twenty? Despite the Parisian decor, the shabby Eiffel Towers in the gold-and-black wallpaper, she was wearing a harem outfit—baggy harem trousers, sheer, transparent, black speckled with gold stars, and a brilliant scarlet sash; nothing at all on top. He stared at her small white breasts, at the pert plum-colored nipples. A girl's. Young. He stared, and looked away in shame; in pity.

Eiffel Tower Topless Body Rub. Parisian Masseuses. Complete Satisfaction Guaranteed. Hours 11 a.m. – 2 a.m. Daily.

$55, plus $5 "towel fee." Had he wanted his hair shampooed it would have been another $5.

Nothing more than a steam bath, really. Sauna. Inexpert massage. Edwin with a plain white towel fixed about his waist, discreetly covering his groin, lying corpse-like on a table, his skin sticking to the vinyl surface. A drink or two beforehand in The Elbow Room a mile away at the downtown Hilton, no appetite for dinner, Friday evening, alone, lonely, what the hell. A kind of joke, really. Not serious. Suppose I drove to Rood Street and spent a few hours there, doing what people do there, what thoughts would I have, would there be consequences . . . ?

Probably not. There never are.

The Eiffel Tower, a few steps down from the sidewalk. Neon

147

tubing. Green-tinted glass, Moorish and Parisian decorations, girls in multi-colored silk sashes, tiny vests which (it turned out) they shed in private, in the private cubicles. Seems rather sad. And barefoot, with toe rings.

I have the idea this is a new job for you, Edwin whispered. You haven't been here long, have you . . . ?

Slapping his back, palms against his shoulder-blades. Distant. No pain. Dull perfunctory bored. Mealy-skinned girl, not pretty. But young. Sad, so young.

I came here tonight out of curiosity, Edwin said. He was beginning to perspire uncomfortably. I'm a free-lance journalist. I was thinking of doing an article on . . . on a typical masseuse. . . . Would you be interested? I mean in an interview. . . .

As the minutes passed he became, oddly, more shy. Did not dare twist about to look at her. (And wasn't there something about keyholes, peep-holes, in these establishments?—one-way mirrors? The proprietor spied on the girls and their customers. Or maybe it was local police who spied. Or other customers who paid extra.)

The steam bath and the massage, such as it was, lasted only about forty-five minutes. $60 for the privilege of sweating and talking into a vaporous abyss, addressing a plain stringy-haired girl who pretended not to hear. What a contemptible fool you are after all, Cynthia giggled.

The shame of it. Humiliation.

But thank God—down here on Rood Street, no one would possibly know.

I came here tonight out of curiosity, Edwin told the manager, paying his bill, smiling genially. If he was upset he gave no sign: remembered to stand erect, stomach in. Still a handsome man. Well-dressed. And the steam bath, no doubt, had freshened his skin; gave his complexion a healthy rosy ruddy glowing look.

Y'all come back, then, the manager said, matching Edwin's

148

smile.

A very fat gnomish man with a humped back, a big onyx ring on one finger, dyed black hair—or was it a wig—teary dark eyes. Womanish face. High-pitched voice.

Y'all come back and see us again soon. Special discount, don't forget, Monday all day.

Never, thought Edwin in a huffy righteous anger.

Pastel lights glaring on a plaster-of-paris fountain, and overhead in a dusty wicker cage a single parakeet—an eerily lovely aqua with white, black, and pale yellow markings. Alive? It twitched, twittered. A single feather detached itself and fell languidly to the bottom of the cage.

Driving home on the northbound Ringer he sees again the girl's wan dissatisfied face, and her small pale breasts, and the lurid scarlet sash. What is your name? I have no name. Would you be interested . . . ? No. No.

A contemptible fool. Revealed at last.

Humble. Humbled.

But very clean! Clean at every pore. . . . For only $60. Plus tax.

I came here out of curiosity, Edwin hears himself say. A need to see, to know. To investigate. No personal interest: really a kind of clinical, sociological investigation. Mores of our contemporary culture. Life-styles. . . . The strange thing is, how well everything at Monarch is going. Should have mentioned it to the masseuse. Monarch Life. Impressive. Vice-president. And with Ralph Geddes in the hospital now there's no competition, there will be clear sailing, ironic that poor Cynthia won't be able to boast of it to her bridge friends, won't even learn of it unless Bushy or Bagot happen to mention the news. But no more than I deserve: working like hell for years. Should have mentioned it to the masseuse.

Y'all come back again real soon, the gnomish creature

149

cooed.

Impertinence. Mock intimacy.

As if he somehow *knew* Edwin. . . .

But no. Not likely. The usual act with customers, clients, whatever they are called, pretense that there has been a transaction of significance, a commitment for the future; the same half-jeering tone up and down the street, no doubt, in the Heart of Darkness Men's Club, in XXX-Rated Books Films & Slides, Rhea's Topless & Bottomless Discotheque, The Ultimate Body Rub & Sauna, The Inner Circle, 10001 Nights, Sodom & Sam's, The Pearl Massage, Milt's Paradise Inne, Wonderland, E-Z's Topless Barbers, Girls Internationale, Bambi's.

Y'all come back again real soon.

Never, whispered Edwin Locke.

XI.

Iris

I've met you, you know, Edwin whispers.
  What?
  I've met you. Before. Elsewhere.
  You have? Where?
  At . . . you know. You know where.
  Where?
  You know.
  No I don't. What the hell are you talking about?
  Now don't get angry, Iris, please. It's just that—
  What the hell do you mean, you've met me? You mean you saw me somewhere, you spied on me or something?
  It isn't important, why don't we—
  Like that day in the bookstore, you spying on me through the shelves of books, is that what you mean? Goddam crazy—
  No I don't mean *that.*
  Then what?
  Nothing. I'm sorry if I upset you.
  You didn't *upset* me, for Christ's sake. How the hell could *you* upset *me.*
  . . . It's just that I met you once before. In March. Four or five weeks ago. You don't remember me but I remember you. We met in . . . in what might be called intimate circumstances.
  Yeah? What intimate circumstances?
  Don't you know?

151

What? Know what?

Iris, please—that hurts.

So what if it hurts?

You wouldn't like me to—

Just try it!

—ow! Stop!

Sooner strangle a child . . . a babe . . . in its crib, than, how does it go, suppress your desires, oh shit, how does it go?

How does what go?

The saying, you asshole! The poetry!

What poetry?

Blake. Something about strangling a baby.

. . . I didn't mean to make you angry, Iris. I'm sorry.

You haven't made me *angry*, Edwin.

I should respect your privacy, your past, I mean if you don't want to remember—that is, if you don't want someone from—from—from *there* to appear in your private life—

There! Where's there!

Oh not far away, only about four or five miles away, isn't it?—The Tower?—an odd name like that, I've forgotten it precisely—or was it The Eiffel Tower—

What's that wink supposed to mean? Jesus Christ—

Iris, wait, don't get up—

I'm not getting up, I'm just getting in a better position to see what the hell's going on here, and this goddam sheet or whatever it is, this pillow, it's all twisted under me; let go, for Christ's sake! Now what the fuck is The Eiffel Tower?

You don't know? Really?

I said—what is it?

The Eiffel Tower, a few miles south of here, in fact it's on Rood, that block behind the Coliseum—you don't know what I mean, really?

Rood? Downtown? That shitty area?

Iris, you're so—

152

Did you say The Eiffel Tower?—what the hell is it?

—so beautiful—

Oh shit, cut it out. I'm not beautiful and I don't give a damn and only an asshole like you from Woodlawn or whatever the hell it is would say such crap. What I want to know is: What's The Eiffel Tower, where do you think we met before?

Iris—

Stop that! I can't stand that wet doggy pleading sick look!

I didn't mean to anger you, dear, I was only—I was only—

Where did we meet before!

—was only teasing.

Edwin Locke, in April, the sweetest of months, strolling with a camera on a strap around his neck, Edwin Locke in a new, rather costly outfit from The Brigidier Men's Shoppe—cajoled into buying it by an enthusiastic salesman who convinced him that the aviator look was not, on his tall strong manly frame, as incongruous as it would be on, say, a man of his age with a less muscular build: catching stealthy reflections of himself in the windows of parked cars and stores, and allowing himself (oh why the hell not! it's April, it's spring, the gay giddy rainbow-wet look of the air is intoxicating!) to feel somewhat pleased. He *does* look young, youngish. He *does* look manly.

A camera. Something fairly lightweight. Not too expensive. Oh a Japanese make, or West German, I'm really just an amateur, just getting started, you know, I don't want to lug around heavy equipment and I don't at the present time have my own—what is it called—developing room, darkroom—Some sort of a shoulder-bag too. Leather. How much? That's a little more than I had intended to pay, but. . . .

Edwin Locke strolling in the bright gay exhilarating sunshine, a few months before his death, has always wanted to be a free-lance journalist or photographer, you know, but don't

153

tell anyone in the office, Edna-Mae, they wouldn't understand. Rood Street as it intersects with Haley. The fringes of the State University campus. Somewhat shabby neighborhood: cheap restaurants, laundromats, dry cleaners, boarded-up stores, Steppenwolf Coffee Shop; Victor Brink for Mayor Headquarters; Les Images Gallery; University Arms Apartments; University Drugs; Giles Prosthetics; Shawnee Chicken Take-out; Legal Aid Center; Women's Caucus for a United Front; Capri New & Used Furniture; Discount Magic & Novelties; James Seeley, Ph.D., Consulting Psychologist & Certified Marriage Counsellor, Sexual Dysfunctions My Specialty; Yamaha Sales & Service; University Optical; Rock-Jazz-Soul Records & Tape Mart; Sybil's Tattooing; Dingley Trophies & Engraving; Campus Typewriter Sales & Service; The New Benares Yoga Center; Rood Sheepskin & Leather; Dotskie Extermination & Fumigation Specializing in Mice Rats Mites Roaches Spiders Silverfish Bees Hornets Ants Bedbugs Carpet Beetles Fleas; Sign of the Zodiac Health Foods; Edward Deal Denture Therapy Clinic; Campus Beer Wine Whiskey; Campus Copying & Duplicating Service; Kim Roy's Chinese Foods Take-Out & Delivery; Haley's Comet New & Used Books Textbooks Magazines Comic Books. Young people everywhere. Some with books, some without. On bicycles. On foot. A jogger—no, two—three joggers running past Edwin, fists and arms swinging, brightly-colored rags tied about their heads, a zany rakish pirate's look, Indian look, attractive. And another jogger—a boy in white shorts, university sweatshirt, maroon with pale gold insignia, or is it a girl?—running with such passion, such little effort, a pleasure to stare after, no envy, no envy, only unabashed frank admiration.

Hello my name is Charles Aulk. Alexander Geller. Clifford Pollock. Howard Diehl. Free-lance journalist. National magazines. Pseudonyms. A series on youth, photographs and commentary. Youth, American, in spring, current trends, life-styles, perhaps a number of interviews, quite casual, conversational, would you be interested?

April. Sweetest of months. Even in the city a certain freshness, unmistakable freshness, to the air. Brief showers, then sunshine. Rainbow curving over distant smokestacks. Roiling clouds, darkly-gray; blown aside to reveal a brilliant blue sky; a long-haired girl on a bicycle, pedalling past, licking an ice cream cone; no envy, no envy.

My mother has invited us to Tucson for two weeks and I have every intention of going, Cynthia said.

But the boys—

The boys *want* to go. They're terribly excited about going. Two weeks of Easter vacation is exactly right and if you try to prevent us they'll be very disappointed, and very angry. You know what a temper Donald is getting.

It's just that I'd planned—

Then change your plans! As I said Mother has invited us to Tucson and she has a friend who owns a ranch, an actual ranch, the boys are counting the days until we leave, I did no more than mention you and they groaned with disappointment, Teddy has been taking books out of the school library, the American Southwest, Indians, pueblos, wild horses, a dude ranch, I wouldn't advise you to contact Bushy on this, I wouldn't advise you to insist upon your rights, if I were you I'd be very very diffident, very cautious, about—

Pouring bourbon into the glass, some distance from the phone, wouldn't want her to hear. Ice cubes tinkling.

You'll pay for this, he whispered.

Edwin? Are you still there?

You'll pay for this! Turning the boys against their father!

Now April. Spring. Once again, spring. Marvelous exhilarating odor. Actual taste to the air. A new suit: aviator sports coat with cuffs that button, pocket with flap that buttons shut, gunmetal-gray trousers, perma-press, quite handsome. Italian shoes, squarish toes, two-inch heels, expensive but worth it, though must avoid puddles because they will stain. Dental canal work finished, some agonizing sessions, best forgotten. Risa's friend's false teeth and capping replaced. *Who on earth did this for you*, Edwin's dentist inquired mildly.

Now April. Klempfheimer Safari Land Camera, Model 15S-49. Fresh roll of film. Only an amateur, driven by curiosity, free-lance article on the opinions . . . the opinions of university students. Politics, morals, sexual behavior. Current fashions. Life-styles. Excuse me, but I wonder if—

No, not that one. Face like curdled milk. Diseased-looking. Might be (who can tell?) a drug addict.

Haley's Comet New & Used Books Textbooks Magazines Comic Books.

Musty odor. Peeling paint: ceiling, walls. Molding filthy. Books everywhere, on metal shelves, on tables, stacked on the floor. Young people in their twenties, sloping shoulders, jeans bleached white, undernourished girl with a baby slung against her shoulder, might be from the Ozarks, meager rodent's face, squinting near-sightedly at a tabloid newspaper, *Action Poetry*.

Hurried telephone call that morning. Gladys? This is Mr. Locke. (A relief, not to have to speak with Edna-Mae.) My sinus trouble seems to be worse, the medication hasn't helped, so I think I'd better. . . . Yes. Right. Have the Brondmuller portfolio typed up, I'll be in tomorrow morning or at least by Thursday. . . . Yes. Right. Fine. *Thanks.*

In the aisle marked *Engineering-English Lit.*, a tall skinny black boy with a maniac's frizzed-out hair is strolling with his arm draped heavily about the frail shoulders of a white girl. Disturbing sight. The boy with a thin black moustache, a pimp's moustache; the girl with her pale blond hair in braids,

156

pouty child-like look, quite pretty. Nothing wrong with Negro and white couples, inter-racial dating, even marriage, even children; but still.

Thin gold chains around the black boy's slender throat. Medals of some sort—religious?—signs of the Zodiac?

On the peeling walls, high above the bookshelves, tattered yellowing posters of Allen Ginsberg, Che Guevera, Marlon Brando as the Godfather, Marx, Lenin, Walt Whitman, Castro, Lee Harvey Oswald, Anaïs Nin, Pogo, Gary Gilmore, Richard M. Nixon, Groucho Marx, Humphry Bogart, Jane Fonda in a spacewoman's outfit, Mick Jagger, Beethoven, Charles Manson, Fritz Perls, Linda Lovelace, Scrooge McDuck, Malcolm X, Janis Joplin. Stacks of old magazines. Fraying newspapers. *Sociology, Economics, History.* From the rear, a flute's limpid notes. Edwin feels unaccountably excited, cannot say why, peers through a corner of the metal shelves at a girl sitting cross-legged in the next aisle. Above her, behind her, *The Social Philosophers from Plato to Marx, A Handbook of Marxist Economics, Revolutionaries of Our Time, The Aesthetics of Anarchy.*

That girl! That face!

Close-set eyes, a small snubbed nose, drab brown hair loose and straggling on her shoulders. Wearing metal-rimmed glasses today. And a shabby peasant shawl, oatmeal-colored and -textured, and the usual blue jeans, and what looks like a man's undershirt.

The masseuse.

Edwin stares, drawing in his breath. Is it—? Really—?

Pasty skin, rather low forehead. Frowning. Moving her lips as she reads. Enviable aplomb there in the aisle, sitting completely relaxed, cross-legged, blocking the way so that customers have to step over her or turn back.

What is she reading? Edwin can't see the cover of the book.

The masseuse. From The Eiffel Tower. That first visit,

weeks ago, nervousness and embarrassment, and afterward the nagging memory: the girl, her cool prim disinterest, her curious self-assurance. (On the second and last visit Edwin drew a much older woman, slack-breasted, surly and ebullient by turns; terribly depressing. Oh God depressing. And as a final blow he *almost* encountered Clifford Geller as he was leaving and Geller was arriving; but each was adroit enough to turn slightly away and not to meet the other's eyes.)

In the aisle, the skinny masseuse in a peasant's shawl, evidently a university student, Edwin stares and stares, swallowing, wondering if she would recognize him. Excuse me, miss, but I'm looking for a book on Marxist economics—oh, don't you work here?—I thought maybe—

Excuse me, miss. I am a free-lance journalist interested in—

Excuse me. We've met before. You *do* remember where?

The girl is taking notes, writing on a clipboard, frowning, quite oblivious of her surroundings. Edwin sees the bookstore manager approaching before she does.

Short youngish man with muttonchop whiskers. Denim jacket.

Hey. You want to buy those books or not?

Calmly the girl raises her eyes. Adjusts her glasses.

Are you talking to me? she asks.

The manager clears his throat. (Is he nervous, Edwin wonders. Edwin is nervous just overhearing the exchange.)

This is a store, not a library. You've been back here an hour. Do you intend to—

I'll be done in a minute, the girl says.

I said this is a store, it isn't a library, you've been sitting there blocking the aisle for an hour, do you—

I'm not hurting your goddam books.

Those books are *for sale*. This isn't a library.

Go fuck yourself, the girl murmurs.

What?

You heard me.

Do you want me to call the police?

All right! I'm done!

She throws down the book she is reading and scrambles to her feet.

Cheap stingy bastard! Selfish—

That's enough, just get out of here.

I didn't hurt your goddam precious books, did I!

And then, trembling, Edwin Locke appears: appears before he has time even to think. How very easily, how very boldly, he steps around the corner and reveals himself and says to the angry manager and the angrier girl, *I'll pay for her books. It isn't necessary to abuse her.*

Abuse her! Iris chortles, hours later. What the hell kind of language was that?

Edwin blushes. Though he is of course pleased.

Iris pays half the rent on a kind of apartment, a kind of artist's loft, in a warehouse building some distance from the university; the other half of her rent is paid by a woman named Zanche, a "wonderful crazy half-genius," a painter and sculptor, who along with her daughter Chrissie shares the loft with Iris. It's a very interesting place, a very . . . large place, Edwin says. But it isn't very private, is it.

There's a lock on the door, Iris says.

Zanche isn't home, nor is Chrissie. Overhead someone is walking heavily—another loft-apartment, another artist?—and the footsteps make Edwin wince. But he is very happy to be here. Very.

I can't believe that happened like that, Iris giggles. That little bastard going to call the police, halfway to the telephone, and somebody steps around and says he'll pay for the books, *it isn't necessary to abuse her!* Oh Christ! Wait till I tell Zanche, wait till I tell Valentin—

They giggle together. Huddle together.

Were you spying on me for long?

Of course not. Not at all.

Oh Jesus the look on his face! Halfway to the telephone to call the police and *you* appear and pull the rug out from under him! The little jerk-off!

It was my pleasure. I was happy to be of service.

She wipes her eyes, her nose. Giggling shrilly. Her thin shoulders shaking. . . . Well. It's like something in a fairy tale or a movie. Or maybe I summoned you, she says, peering at him quizzically through her glasses.

Maybe you did, Edwin whispers.

XII.

Zanche. Chrissie.

"Is she back again? Is that miserable little—I mean that over-grown *thing!*—is she back again already?"

The child, moon-faced, expressionless, halts just inside the doorway. Edwin waves her away. Go on, go on, don't get your mother angry again, *go on,* you poor sad creature—

"Is she back? I heard her on the stairs—heard *someone*—heavy-footed as an elephant—"

"It's all right, Zanche," Edwin calls out, with an air of self-assurance, an air, even, of jocularity, which he doesn't exactly feel. "She's all right."

"Chrissie? Are you back already? What happened to the other kids?"

The child, ungainly and apprehensive, with her characteristic look of queer, soulless, half-witted and yet *cunning* audacity, remains standing just inside the doorway, not exactly hiding, not cringing, while Zanche, barefoot in front of her oversized canvas, against the farther wall of the flat, shouts toward her and Edwin. "You get back downstairs! Get outside! You've been mooning around here all winter and it's spring now! It's a warm sunny healthy day! Do you hear me? Do you? Get outside and play with those kids, aren't Steffie's girls there, I thought you *liked* them, for God's sake won't you make an effort to be normal? —Is she still there, Edwin? Is she there?"

161

"Go on back outside," Edwin mutters. "Chrissie, please. Your mother is very—"

"If I put this brush down and come over there, if I get hold of that homely little frog-faced brat—"

Edwin tries to usher the child out onto the landing. "It's a lovely day, Chrissie honey, isn't it?—why are you back upstairs already? Your mother is worried about you, she wants you to get some fresh air and sunshine, you know how nervous she becomes when you run around the flat—"

The child makes a whimpering noise behind her hand. Her colorless pig-like eyes narrow.

"Yes? What?"

Edwin leans over her though he feels, as always, uneasy in her presence. He is afraid—afraid—of what?—that the girl will try to hug him, that she will press her pale fat face against him, blubbering? (She does not cry as other children do: she blubbers. Tears stream down her plump quivering cheeks, her nose runs alarmingly, her rather gross features threaten to dissolve and trickle earthward. An ugly child, Edwin thinks helplessly. But then, as always, a moment later he thinks: No she's attractive. In her own way. In her own very special way.)

"What is it, Chrissie? Are the other children bothering you?"

She nods emphatically. But does that mean yes?—or—?

"Why don't you play by yourself, then," Edwin whispers. He pushes her toward the stairs; she moves sluggishly, reluctantly. Making that dull whining noise deep in her throat, like a wounded, baffled animal. "Here's a dollar. Okay? Put it in your pocket, dear. Yes. Here, let me. See? It's in your shirt pocket for safekeeping. Yes, right here—*here.* Now I wouldn't necessarily show it to the other children, I mean right away, but you could kind of—oh, you know—after a while, maybe—you could suggest some ice cream or popsicles and tell them you'll treat—do you understand? You do? All right.

162

Fine. But don't mention it immediately, just be casual about it. And try not to bother your mother, Chrissie, when she's working. You know how agitated she gets—"

The child makes an impatient guttural sound. "Nnnnnyahhhh."

"Your mother loves you, she loves you very much, but there are times when— Well, you see, she's very high-strung, she's unusually sensitive, she's an artist—even *I* don't understand her all the time—so we have to be considerate of her, don't we? Of her moods. So if you could play outside until, oh around dinner time I should think, or if you get tired maybe Steffie would let you nap in her place—you've done that before, haven't you? Yes? It would help your mother, you know. And me. Because things are difficult at the present time. You can't understand, I suppose, but you can probably *sense* . . . you can probably sense that things are difficult right now, can't you?"

She blinks at him, suspiciously. Despite the blandness of her moon face—which is neither a girl's face, nor a boy's—simply a *face*—there is something secretive, almost wicked, about her gaze.

From the flat comes Zanche's despairing voice: "What's going on? Is she in trouble? Did she hurt herself?"

"She's all right," Edwin shouts. "She's fine."

"Did she hurt herself?"

"I said she's fine, she's going back outside, there's no trouble at all."

Chrissie turns, groping for the railing. Her mother's voice has evidently frightened her off: thank God. Edwin has an impulse to run his hand through her coarse snarled hair, maybe to squeeze her neck, warmly, paternally, but he resists. He has rarely touched the child, and then only by accident.

As if sensing his thoughts she breaks away suddenly, chortling. Runs down the stairs. Heavy-footed, yes, as an elephant. A baby elephant.

163

"For God's sake, Chrissie," Edwin cries, "be careful. Do you want to fall and—"

But she ignores him. Is probably no longer aware of him. Running downstairs, hitting the steps with her heels, making the old building shudder. Hadn't she fallen a few months ago, hadn't the poor thing broken her ankle, or sprained it? Edwin has a dim vague memory of the child with her foot in a cast. A filthy white cast. Iris introduced him one confused evening to Zanche, and huddling behind Zanche was that strange child, her foot in a cast, her pale loose lips quivering damply.

Ah. Your daughter.

Of course she's my daughter! Don't you see the family resemblance?

Why yes I suppose I—

Why yes!

Hands on her bony hips, chin out-thrust. Black hair streaked unevenly with gray, fairly crackling about her face, taut with electricity. Staring at him. A woman in her mid-thirties, perhaps, with the lean angular tense body of a young boy.

What did I say to offend her, Edwin asked Iris when they were alone. She seemed so angry, suddenly. . . .

Oh because of the kid.

What? What about the kid?

Because, you know, she's a little slow. Retarded, I guess.

Is she?

Well—I don't know. I mean I'm not certain, Zanche doesn't talk about personal things, it isn't any of my business. I try to keep out of her way as much as possible.

But hasn't the child been tested? Surely she goes to school, doesn't she?

Oh I don't think so, anyway not recently. She's always kind of sick. Respiratory trouble. The winter I moved in, the poor kid had pleurisy, I think her lung collapsed or something—

164

isn't that what happens, with pleurisy? And then she's always falling, too. Hitting her head.

Does Zanche take her to the doctor?

Oh she's all right now. The cast is supposed to come off soon.

She has such a heavy-hearted melancholy look. . . .

Like I say, I try to keep out of Zanche's way as much as possible, especially when she's on the war-path. I pay half the rent but—well, never mind. I mean, I pay *half*, you'd think I would be entitled to half of the flat, but she's got her goddam stuff spread out everywhere, you saw it, I refuse to fight, I feel sorry for the kid too, I'm not going to get mixed up in anything. So she falls down, she falls *down*. I'm not telling any tales to the police or Children's Aid or whatever you call it.

Where is her father?—Zanche's husband?

Oh for Christ's sake, Iris said, sputtering with laughter, *Zanche's husband!* Get a load of you!

Doesn't she have a father?

Father, shit. She's had fathers. And plenty of them.

But—

But nobody recently. On account of Zanche has scared them all away, I think permanently; you can't blame them, can you? Oh she's a wonderful person, a kind of crazy woman, but a genius—I really mean it, wait till you see her work—not that big Styrofoam thing by the window, that isn't hers—she's what you would call an original personality. You know—unique.

She certainly does seem very—very outspoken.

Oh she comes on kind of hostile, she's always like that with people I bring home, you know, guys, she's kind of suspicious of them, in fact she's suspicious of *me*. Like a big sister or something. But she doesn't mean it, actually. It's just that she's sensitive about her daughter.

Did she think I was staring, or—?

165

Who knows what she thinks! Who cares!

It's just that she seemed so angry, it was rather upsetting—

Hey. You should know, Zanche was actually *interested* in you. Don't misinterpret her.

What do you mean, Edwin asked, blushing.

What do I mean!

She certainly seemed—

Oh the hell what she *seemed*. I know the woman inside and out, and you don't.

Chrissie. Poor Chrissie, Edwin often thinks. Nine years old and the size of an eleven- or twelve-year-old. Fatherless.

Does she make you nervous, hulking around like that? Zanche asks.

Of course not. No.

You're lying. You're being polite.

No, actually—

Go in the bedroom, Chrissie, for God's sake. Turn on the television. Or go out on the landing—go *somewhere*. We're trying to relax and have a beer and a smoke and you're *hulking* and depressing the hell out of us. Go on!

Actually, Zanche, she's no trouble—

She *is!* She *is* trouble! Her middle name is trouble!

Clumsy chunky sexless body. The soft pale face expressionless as a foam rubber, except—occasionally—for a coy sly unnerving grin. At times her complexion is yellowish. A coarse melancholy yellow. Liverish yellow. Strange, strange. Very strange.

You should try, Edwin says gently, to love your daughter more. After all she can't help the way she is.

—Which is exactly what drives me wild, Zanche shouts.

Edwin Locke. Zanche. And Chrissie.

Half his life at Monarch and Place Rivière. The other half,

166

including his new wardrobe, at Zanche's. Of course he pays all the rent, pays for the utilities, groceries, Zanche's art supplies (which are extraordinarily expensive). Let me for God's sake buy you a new refrigerator, Edwin says in exasperation; the old one, a pullman model, is inefficient, and gives off an odor of compost. Why the hell should we give those fuckers the satisfaction, Zanche says. I *hate* mechanical things.

1616 Cray Street. Warehouse district. A block from the Bowie Expressway, noisy and fume-ridden during working hours, deserted after dark. A dangerous area, people will say, after Edwin Locke's ugly death, but in fact it isn't particularly dangerous—youth gangs don't bother with the area because no one lives there except for the impoverished "artists" colony on Cray Street, and an uncalculated number of vagrants and rummies who get occasional meals at the Rood Street Mission or the Salvation Army headquarters nearby. From early in the morning until late afternoon there are trucks everywhere, going and coming, loading and unloading, and the thought has crossed Edwin's mind that perhaps Chrissie—though she *is* nine years old, and fairly astute in many ways—shouldn't play out on the sidewalk. Or wherever she plays. Or does she "play" at all? —Maybe I could drive her up to the zoo, Edwin suggests, timorously. Or we could all go out to Lighthouse Point sometime, and—

And what? Spoil her?

But just for a change of scene—

She's happy enough here. She never complains.

It's true that she never complains, but—

Look, my friend, Zanche says patiently, other people have taken pity on her too. *The poor little thing! She seems so sad! She never smiles, does she?—poor mistreated creature!* Valentin Rok, my former associate, played daddy for a while, for as long as it amused him; then he lost interest. He's here a while, then he's gone. What the hell—you know *I* don't give a damn, I don't even mind his stuff lying around here—and the Styrofoam thing is pretty good, I think, there are mornings when it really inspires me—no matter what other people think—there are some *very* jealous characters living in this building, you know—but—anyway—Rok pretended to like her, sang songs to her, gave her some goddam Russian Easter eggs or something, when he was high he was particularly affectionate—with her, I mean, not with *me*—the bastard— then suddenly he'd lose interest, and when she came crowding around him, the poor thing is always *hulking*, sort of *looming*, it even got to the point where he'd shove her away. Hey Zanche call your daughter off, he'd say. The bastard. And once he slapped her—he's a mean drunk, and he slapped her, and I don't allow that—and I slapped *him*—and he swung on me and knocked me down, split my lip, would have kicked me in the face but I was too fast for him, I rolled away and hid under the table, that table right there. So. You see. The kinds of bastards that have played daddy to the poor kid and then turned against her—!

But Zanche, Edwin protests, you can't think that *I*—

And your little sweetheart Iris, too. She went through a phase when she first moved in. Playing mommy. (She and Rok—did they really think I didn't know about the two of them?—did they really think I gave a damn what they did when I wasn't here?) She'd had some kind of abortion, one of those late, dangerous ones, the sixth month or something, the fetus is practically *bawling* by then, so naturally she wanted to make amends, she talked herself into thinking she *loved* poor Chrissie, could even work up tears, let them run down her cheeks, it was very touching, it was probably very therapeutic. Chrissie would break something or get into my paints, deliberately to annoy me, and naturally I would discipline her, and she'd run screaming to Iris, who'd hold her and baby her and say Now there, now there, your mommy doesn't mean to be so nasty, your mommy isn't always in her right mind, that kind of shit which I don't need to tolerate, especially not from a foul-mouthed little bitch of a hypocrite who hands over a check for her half of the month's rent and then takes off for—where the hell was it last time—Marrakech—and sure enough the check bounces and who has to make up the difference? Good old Zanche. Good old Earth Mother Zanche. So once the kid burnt herself fooling around with the tea kettle, which I had forbidden her to get anywhere near, she's so clumsy, and she's screaming and screaming, and that little dear Iris threatens to go to the police, she says there's some kind of child abuse law, you can turn people in, people in your own family, even, you can inform on them anonymously, and nobody can sue for false arrest or anything: *anyway:* so I asked her what the hell is this, blackmail?—and she said with a straight face she only had Chrissie's interests at heart, she was *afraid* for Chrissie's life, all that kind of shit which just drives me wild, I mean you can only tolerate so much of it, people who don't know anything about the situation playing mommy and daddy, and hinting that you're a failure as a mother—!

Edwin clutches at the woman's flailing despairing hands.

I certainly didn't—didn't mean—

All of you are driving me crazy, I swear you're pushing me toward doing something terrible!

But Zanche, you can't think that I meant—I only suggested taking Chrissie out of the city for a few hours—you can't possibly link me with those others—you know I love you—

Oh bugger off!

I love you—

Bugger off, goddam you! *I don't even know who you are!*

Edwin Locke. 1616 Cray Street. A new life. A new half-life. No one at Monarch knows, of course; nor do any of Edwin's

169

friends, nor his former neighbors. Occasionally he plays handball at the Athletic Club and it's a temptation, a real temptation, to tell Charles Diehl or Joe Bushy or Floyd McKay: I am living with a woman of great passion, a woman who has lived, who has suffered, an artist, a possible genius, a woman of the sort I've never encountered before, and men like you know nothing about. *Nothing.*

1616 Cray Street. Less than forty-five minutes from Monarch Life on the southbound Ringer and the westbound Bowie. Only a half-mile from the Marcher Street exit of the Bowie Expressway—really quite convenient. Someday you'll have to show me your office building and your office, Zanche says. I'd like to see you there. At your desk. Ordering your secretaries around. Talking to New York, Boston, Los Angeles. The real thing, eh? I could sketch you there, maybe do a painting. Someday. I insist.

Half his life at Monarch and Place Rivière; the other half at 1616 Cray Street. Dizzying, the change. The contrast. Look at the sort of woman I'm worthy of, Edwin whispers to Cynthia. You wouldn't recognize your husband now!

First there was Iris. Charming, rather unreliable Iris. You know I wouldn't lie to you, Edwin, she protested, her lips primly pursed. You know I wouldn't lie because I respect you too much. (Had she worked at The Eiffel Tower? Edwin didn't know. Really didn't know. She was not a university student though she "had plans" to go to night school someday and major in psychology; she would admit to no background at all. The books Edwin bought for her at Haley's Comet were not Marxist studies but books on the occult—*Secrets of Lost Atlantis, UFO's: The God Who Walks Among Us, Witchcraft Black and White.*)

First there was Iris. Then one day in late April Edwin arrived at 1616 Cray and Zanche opened the door and said with a bemused twist of her lips that Iris was gone—had left that morning with a friend on a Pan American flight to Guadalajara, Mexico. Had left, in fact, owing Zanche money.

How—how much? Edwin asked automatically.

The next day he gave Zanche a darkly translucent onyx in a silver setting, to wear around her neck on a chain. Though she never wore it—I detest things around my neck, in fact jewelry of all kinds, she said—she kept it close by, on her cluttered work-table, or on her bureau, or bed; or on top of the refrigerator. She kept it close by while she worked so that, for good luck, she might rub it against her cheek or throat or breasts. An odd, charming woman, to be so superstitious!

First Iris, whose meager beauty quickly faded; and then Zanche, bold clever deft daring impatient passionate Zanche, the most extraordinary woman Edwin Locke ever knew. Do you see who loves me now, Edwin whispered to Cynthia.

Love love love love love.

1616 Cray Street. A former Mayflower warehouse. Rodent-infested, poorly-heated, never inspected by the city Board of Health, officially vacant. In reality inhabited by ten or twelve or fifteen persons, most of whom claimed to be artists, all of whom were on welfare or unemployment compensation. Steffie and Terry and Mike and D.B. and Lim Ch'ung. And of course Zanche and little Chrissie.

Zanche's apartment was on the third floor—an "apartment" that was only one large room and one closet-like bedroom without a window. The ceiling was fifteen feet high, and made of hammered tin. Crossing one another at fanciful intervals on the bare floorboards were carpet remnants of various colors. There were exposed pipes, high narrow cupboards without doors, a two-burner gas range, an old pullman refrigerator, a badly-stained aluminum sink, a dirt-encrusted shower stall in a corner of the kitchen. (A communal toilet, unspeakably filthy, was located out in the corridor.) Some shabby old pieces of furniture—two chairs, a settee, a floor-lamp with a fringed shade—and ashtrays piled high with ashes and butts and apple cores—and Zanche's canvases, paints, brushes, rags, Coke bottles, sketch pads, jars of turpentine. Everywhere, the sobering stink of turpentine.

Can't you open the skylight a little, Edwin asked one day.

What? Why?

The turpentine—

What turpentine?

The air's a little close in here, I was just thinking it might be more pleasant if—

What's wrong? Is something wrong?

Nothing's wrong. Except the turpentine odor, don't you find it a little—

Her dark eyes rolled harshly in their sockets. He saw, to his astonishment, that the woman was *hurt*.

No, it's all right, it's really all right, he said. I realize that Chrissie is susceptible to colds. I realize that now.

Paper towels, paint-smeared tissues, Chrissie's cotton socks and cotton panties, old newspapers. In the corners, under the sink, rodent droppings. Cobwebs. Dirt-encrusted molding. Bare lightbulbs operated by switches. Near the skylight (which, though covered with a thin film of dirt, throws a vivid, violent glare upon everything in the main room) the nine-foot-high sculpture left behind by a former lover, Valentin Rok: *Hamlet*, the thing is called, playfully or not Edwin does not know. What is he to think of it? How is he to assess it? Zanche claims the "sculpture" is brilliant but all Edwin sees is a bloated mass, misshapen as a tumor, made of Styrofoam, strips of plastic and glass, brick chips, twine, string, strands of Zanche's and Chrissie's hair, even, according to Zanche, cuttings from Rok's toenails. A bearded sculptor in his forties, Zanche's downstairs neighbor D.B., has said that *Hamlet* is marred by Rok's Russian superficiality—it appears to be bold and revolutionary but is, in fact, cripplingly conser-

172

vative. On the other hand Zanche's friend Steffie—not a practicing artist at the present time, but a former painter, and a former night school teacher at the City Center Fine Arts League—has insisted in Edwin's presence that *Hamlet* is "probably a work of genius," "probably the first authentic harbinger of the twenty-first century."

Rok won't like the fact that you're here, Steffie told Edwin one night. Even if he did walk out on her.

Gay, giddy, floating Edwin Locke would only whisper with numbed lips: You can't frighten me. My life is within my grasp at last and *you can't frighten me.*

□ □ □

At his desk, floating above the gaseous expressway. Mists, clouds, coils of smoke. Vice-president. Mr. Locke. As efficient as ever. Hurried but careful. Cautious. Thinking of Zanche and what they have done together, what they will do together. Her knees locked behind his buttocks. Oh love. Oh my God. Oh I don't think I can bear it.

Never so alive before. Never so *living*.

Zanche with the smooth black stone between her breasts, her bluish eyelids closed. Sexual exhaustion. Depletion.

And Chrissie—does Chrissie know?

Does she eavesdrop? Peek?

If Iris should return—

Iris's pipe (which they have used freely, stuffed with first-rate hashish, a gift of D.B.'s) passed from one to the other to the other. Should Iris return unexpected she will take the pipe and draw in the heavy sweetly-acrid smoke and her eyes will roll upward and everyone will laugh with delight. Zanche and Iris and Edwin. Edwin and Zanche. And Iris. Sleepwalkers. Unhurried. Am I the person who is doing these things, Edwin wonders, amazed. But no: it is I to whom these things are

173

being done. I myself am innocent. Guiltless.

Poor little Chrissie. No father. Sleeping in that narrow cot, on those grimy sheets. Is she slow-witted—or only pretending? Perhaps she knows more than she lets on. Nine years old but so tall, so softly plump. A moon face. Expressionless. Yellowish skin, bad teeth. Coarse snarled hair. (I can't get a comb through it, I've given up, Zanche sighs, waving the child away. Get lost!) A thick torso, thick thighs, knees. Freakish? Oh perhaps. Slightly. The other children are quick and cruel: Loony, Dopey, Dum-Dum, Goof.

Poor thing.

Fatherless.

Don't cry, your mother doesn't mean it, your mother is feeling nervous today, Edwin whispers, stroking the child's neck, peering into her dull expressionless fascinating eyes. Sometimes an ordinary brown, sometimes a queer tawny gold. How much does she know? What is reflected, what is registered, in her sleepy brain?

Her bouts of giggling, which are sometimes convulsive. And those dismaying sobs. And those hours of emptiness, complete silence, void. She can sit for minutes at a time without moving, she can stare at her mother's quick tireless arm as she paints, showing no emotion, not even a flicker of apprehension when Zanche turns to her at last. You make me nervous sitting there, why don't you go lie down and nap, why don't you play outside, isn't there *anything* for you to do! Blinking slowly, her pale lips parted and damp. Can she sense, Edwin wonders, the odd note of aggrieved pleasure in Zanche's voice . . . ? Can she sense, despite Zanche's frequent exasperated slaps and blows, the woman's love for her?

Maybe if you sent her to school, Edwin suggested once. The problem is, I think, you and she are too much together. . . .

And have her bullied? Laughed at? Pushed around?

But I don't think that would necessarily happen. I mean, if

174

she were sent to a special school. . . .

It's too far. The bus ride is too long. Anyway those kids are worse: those retarded kids are animals. And she isn't one of them, anyway. She's just slow. Sometimes it's deliberate. You don't know her the way I do, you don't understand the subtleties in her behavior, the tricks, the little ploys. . . . Isn't that right, kid? Eh? See, she's been listening to all this! She doesn't miss a thing, do you?

Moony-faced. Square-bodied. Lethargic. Only nine years old and already she has tiny breasts—like inverted paper cups, so small. And yet: there is something unnatural about them, Edwin thinks uneasily, they are the sort of fleshy growths one sometimes sees in plump men and boys, males who are not altogether *male*.

Poor child. . . .

At his enormous teakwood desk he sits, high in the Monarch Life Building, staring at the featureless sky. Am I the person who is doing these things? . . . Actually he is working very hard this spring. Very hard. So that no one will suspect. So that there will be no cause, absolutely no cause, for vicious rumors to circulate about him.

He sits, he dreams. Ponders. His heart, that strong muscle, beats with assurance. There is Zanche, there is Chrissie, there is Edwin Locke. There is even an absent love named Valentin Rok. (But someone told someone who told Zanche, rather irresponsibly, that Rok has been seen in town—but of course it could be a false rumor. Anyway I'm through with that sadistic bastard, Zanche says, except on a professional basis: I mean, I respect him as an artist. But not as a man. Not as a man who has any claim on *me*.)

There is Edwin, there is Zanche. The woman he has waited all his life to meet. Flamboyant, crude, short-tempered Zanche with her strong angular features, her accusing stare, her amazing energy. It tires him simply to watch her work.

175

How insubstantial his other women are, set beside her!

The average woman, Edwin thinks, isn't completely real. Doesn't *exist*.

Zanche and her large splotched canvases. She has been working for months in muted, somber shades—mauve, gray, olive-green, a soiled white—and her brush-strokes have been bold and coarse. He cannot assess her art. He stares, and cannot really *see*. (Years ago Cynthia mocked his conservatism: Why must everything be literal, simply so that *you* can make sense of it! Artists don't care about *you*, Edwin, they don't make people like you the measure of their art.)

Zanche and her paint-stained hands. Her clothes that smell of turpentine. The smooth black stone turned in her nervous fingers, rubbed absent-mindedly against her cheek and throat. My love? My fierce triumphant mistress.

Do you see what my life is now, Edwin asks Cynthia, do you see how far I've travelled from you . . . ?

Swine, Cynthia whispers.

XIII.

Sussex Lane

And *you.* Self-righteous unfeeling complacent manipulative prig, Edwin whispers.

Liar. Murderer.

She does not hear. Does not pause. The impersonal but chatty voice explaining the circumstances behind her most recent strategems: putting the house on the market, buying a condominium in Woodland Village Estates, arranging for Donald to start in September at The Georges Fenkell Academy in Dorchester, Massachusetts, arranging for poor Teddy to start therapy twice a week with Dr. Myron Kornbloom the prominent, and very expensive, children's psychiatrist whose office is in that striking square building of pleated concrete adjacent to The Round Table.

Don't you care for my advice?—didn't you pause to ask yourself what *I* might—

The telephone voice remote yet not unfriendly. A woman. A woman's voice. Acquaintance of his? Telling him about someone named Hockney—no, not poor *Edgar*—who is evidently running for the Democratic nomination for governor. Reform wing of the party. Badly needed. Mainly younger men and women. Canvassing, public relations work, arranging for Hockney to visit clubs, professional organizations, PTA groups, local television interview shows, universities throughout the state. Already, Cynthia assures him in a

177

breathy, excited voice, that corrupt old buzzard Shandy is having second thoughts about running for reelection.

Is he. That's very—

"I think what happened, Edwin," Cynthia says after a brief pause, "was that I tired suddenly of the inconsequential life I was leading. All that emotion. All that thinking about emotion. A few weeks ago I woke up and there was a sort of blank, an absence, in my mind . . . and I realized it was the area you used to inhabit. I no longer hated you. Or even disliked you. I suppose I felt pity for you, but even that is fading, and my life is so altered now that I don't even have time for *that*. Most of all I feel pity for the person I'd been for so many years, not just during our marriage but before it too. For most of my life, in fact. . . . My God, Edwin, just imagine: that you once had the power to upset me so much, I'd even been thinking of suicide for a while!"

"Suicide? Oh but Cynthia, did you really? I mean I— I didn't know—"

But the calm frank friendly voice continues uninterrupted: "So I just got bored suddenly. With the triviality of my concerns. With my daily life. The telephone calls from Bushy and Bagot, and the letters, and fuss about the boys, and bridge luncheons, and drinking too much in the afternoon, and crying, and feeling sorry for myself, and exchanging bad news with certain friends of mine whose husbands are also—well, whose marriages are undergoing radical transformations. I just got suddenly weary of it all."

"Friends? Which friends? Is it—"

"So I went down to Hockney's headquarters and volunteered to help and I've been working between eight and twelve hours a day, sometimes even on Sundays, and everything has changed completely. I know you're probably skeptical—you never had any interest in the community, or in anything much beyond yourself—but my life has been transformed. I'm

178

not the Cynthia you used to know. I'm hardly even the boys' mother—as they've begun to realize finally. (And it's been good for *them* too.) At first Teddy seemed to regress rather alarmingly, and Donald tried his silent routine with me, but then they realized I wouldn't play the game any longer, I wouldn't succumb to their blackmail, and things have worked out surprisingly well. And Donald is actually looking forward to boarding school in September."

"How much is the tuition, again? I didn't exactly get the figure—"

"I just tired, you see, of being inconsequential. Of thinking about three or four silly empty things day after day. After all, Edwin, our marriage was a mistake: and the best thing to do about a mistake, even one that took such a big chunk out of my life, is to forget it, and move on. Don't you agree? The years with you were like an ocean crossing, a very long crossing, they haven't bound us together for life and I see now that I was naive to think they could, and to be angry with you for disappointing me. After all—you can't be to blame for *my* delusion!"

"Cynthia, tell the truth—*is* there another man? I only want to—"

"So I've made a down payment on a two-bedroom condominium in Woodland Village, and I've put the house on the market; and things are gradually taking shape, becoming simplified. I want to get rid of *clutter*. As far as my work with Hockney goes—of course we're all delighted about Shandy's decision (it's only a rumor at the present time, but we have it on good authority that it's probably true) but at my age I'm too wise to be really idealistic. If Hockney wins the nomination—fine. If not I'll accept that too. I don't think I have the capacity, Edwin, even to be disillusioned any longer, and it's a wonderfully liberating feeling. Which I owe to you. Really. To you, and the divorce, and all those stormy unbearable months. . . . Yes, even if Hockney runs and wins and turns out to be less admirable than some of us think: I'll accept that too. But I don't think I'm naive to believe that with him things will be *somewhat* better in the party, and in state politics. Did you know that since Moody took office the Highway Commission alone has given out contracts amounting to—"

Prig. Liar. *Murderer.*

Memory of her tear-stained face. Ugly distorted mouth. Eyes bloodshot, reddened. You can't mean it, what are you saying, did you say . . . divorce? Oh Edwin you can't mean it! She loved me then. Loved me.

Sussex Lane. Mid-summer. A pleasantly warm Sunday afternoon. Edwin in his air-conditioned car (but the air-conditioning is not so efficient as it once was: should take it in for a check-up), parked across the street from his house, contemplating the *Magnus Realtors For Sale* sign, tasteful white and green, but a jarring sight nonetheless.

Jarring too, and alarming, is the fact that the house is already vacant. He hadn't known, or at any rate doesn't remember being told, that Cynthia and the boys were moving out so soon. Are they already in the condominium? Or have they gone out to Cynthia's mother's again? Edwin lights another of the thin cigars, though the taste of the tobacco is rather nauseating; he tells himself it will be good for him, will help, like the whiskey, to calm his nerves. Something is going on, something very sinister and underhanded and manipulative, and he doesn't quite know what it is. But he dare not telephone Bagot again, after that argument the other week. . . .

Handsome house: gray shingles, red shutters, impressive slate roof (a genuine slate roof, not like the shoddy imitations that have begun to appear on even the expensive "executive" homes in the area). But is the sprinkler system faulty again?

The grass is beginning to burn out in spots. Edwin stares. Sadly. Like what's-his-name rolling the rock up the hill, and then it rolls back down again, trying to keep a decent lawn, trying to keep things looking good . . . and you can see quite plainly where the Maccabee's lawn begins.

Embarrassing. Almost criminal of Cynthia to move out.

And to take the boys away with her!

Won't you talk to Daddy over the phone, he begs, but Teddy has run off and hidden. (In the basement. Behind the furnace.) Don't you want to get together for a baseball game this Saturday?—but Donald has a music lesson, has other plans. If he'd had a daughter things would be different. Altogether different. He would be linked more closely, more *meaningfully*, with . . . with life, with the earth itself. Cynthia hadn't wanted to try again, for a girl. Or perhaps he hadn't wanted to at the time. Tragic loss. If only he had a daughter. . . .

A little short of breath from the cigar. He pours himself an inch or two in the paper cup, just to clear his thoughts.

If only. . . .

What has he been thinking of . . . ?

Long thin acrid-tasting Peruvian cigars. Cigarillos. An impulsive gesture, Valentin Rok giving him a handful the other night: of course he could not refuse. And Rok meant nothing by it, nothing ironic or condescending.

Isn't he an extraordinary person, Zanche whispered. Of course he's monstrous and I detest him and even fear him, a little, but still you must admit. . . .

Must I, thinks Edwin sadly.

They met, finally, Edwin and Rok, a week ago Saturday night, in the studio-flat of a friend of Zanche's, in the very building in which Zanche and Chrissie lived. A meeting engineered by Zanche's "friends"—to embarrass and upset her, or to embarrass and upset Edwin—or simply to provide a bit of drama, or a few minutes' diversion?—probably there was no

181

malice intended. Just gaiety, high spirits, exuberance. Everyone was very drunk.

Zanche and Edwin came late to the party since Chrissie had thrown one of her tantrums. And had to be given, forcibly, her whiskey-and-milk—otherwise she'd never sleep, would escape from the flat and prowl around the building and possibly even end up at the party, which was held in Steffie's studio on the first floor, at the rear. So they came late, though they were already fairly high, in fact Edwin's skull was buzzing, and there—there was Valentin Rok, as familiar to Edwin as if he'd seen the man before, though in fact no one had even described him in much detail.

Valentin Rok!—not so tall as Edwin had imagined, no more than 6'3 or 4. Silvery hair that fell to his shoulders. An actor's broad oversized face—or perhaps it was slightly Mongolian, Oriental—flattened and balloon-like and high-colored. Not handsome. Not at all. Imposing, impressive, striking—but not handsome. Even rather ugly. A hook nose, and an uneven beard, and moist dark slightly bulging eyes, and lips that were too full and too red. High on amphetamines and beer, they said, but unusually good-humored: look at the way he rushed to poor terrified Zanche and embraced her, and tried, even to embrace Edwin, shouting with laughter, calling them *My dear sister, my dear brother.* And lapsing frequently into what Edwin assumed was Russian. *You must not shrink from me, we must be friends, we must acknowledge one another's right to exist here on earth . . . !*

Noisy party. Exuberant uninhibited people. Gaiety, laughter, amplified electronic music, friends of Zanche's, fellow-tenants of 1616 Cray, friends of friends, strangers. Edwin quite excited. Edwin quite dazed. Steffie . . . and Little Joey . . . and D.B. and his girl, a skinny little thing with a glazed moronic look . . . and Lim Ch'ung the welder-sculptor . . . and Terry . . . and Max . . . and Josephine . . . and. . . . Edwin happened to see

182

two tiny faces peering down at them all from a far corner of the room. Steffie's twins, a girl and a boy, put to bed for the night in their rather unusual little room—not a room exactly but a sort of large box made of untreated lumber, the size of a kennel. It was an oddity of carpentering that Edwin, who had seen it before, had never comprehended. It was built into the corner of the room, up against the ceiling, and must have had some function when the place was used as a warehouse; now it made a clever, though rather cramped, bedroom for the twins. During the day a straight ladder was set against its square-cut door, but at night the ladder was usually taken away so that the twins could not get down into the studio and prowl around. They were six years old and unusually inquisitive for their age. And a great deal of trouble, Steffie said.

Valentin Rok was the center of attention. He told of his recent adventures in Peru as the companion and body-guard of a wealthy man, an Italian nobleman whose name Rok dared not reveal; in his knapsack he had pictures—they turned out to be superb photographs, impressive even to Edwin's untrained eye—of the slums of Lima, the Pacific coast, the Andes, the rain forests. As Rok gestured, throwing his beringed hands about, shaking his silvery hair impatiently out of his perspiring face, Edwin stared, and stared, and though he had wisely stopped drinking he could not halt the progress of an uncanny, overwhelming intoxication. Rok's gleaming face, Rok's muscular shoulders and arms, his thin, saffron-colored peasant's shirt, the heavy necklace of hammered silver he wore rather tightly against his throat, above all Rok's high gloating indefatigable voice which mesmerized his listeners—Edwin stared, transfixed, and felt suddenly that he was very close to the edge.

How it came about, or why, he could not tell. Nor could he comprehend it afterward. But he stood there paralyzed. Staring. Listening. On the brink of terror. As if the world might

183

suddenly burst open. As if the universe itself, kept always at a discreet distance, might suddenly burst upon him and annihilate him utterly. *Oh my God don't let*—

The humiliation of that Saturday night was to come later, in fact hours later, but Edwin remembered Rok most clearly when he was telling Zanche and Steffie and D.B. and Joey and Lim Ch'ung and the others about his Peruvian adventures. The voice, the glistening face, the red lips, the busy maddening hands.... The human soul isn't prepared to absorb so much, Edwin thought helplessly, going for another drink.

Sussex Lane. A dim tug of nostalgia. Should feel more, should feel *loss*. But only the irritation with Cynthia and the obscure embarrassment on account of the lawn. By mid-August it will be burnt-out completely and Howard Maccabee will be making comments about slovenly neighbors. And the shutters will need paint soon. And the black-top drive appears to be cracking in spots.

What the hell, Edwin thinks, sighing. He pours himself another drink, staring into the paper cup. Around his neck are several thin gold chains; weighing rather heavily on his nose is a pair of plastic-framed sunglasses with very dark lenses. His lime-green nylon sports shirt is opened to the third button, showing a modest expanse of tanned chest. (He and Zanche were sunbathing the other day, on the warehouse roof. Naked. They finished a bottle of red wine, dozed off, and woke an hour and a half later, almost *too* tanned.) . . . Is that Maccabee himself, fussing in the rhododendron bed alongside his house? Edwin isn't sure if he wants to be recognized.

Yet it would take too much effort to drive away. He feels unaccountably tired. The house, his former neighbors' houses, the stumps of the old elm trees, the porous, layered look of the summer sky itself: he sits lazily mesmerized, sipping at this drink, staring. A quiet Sunday. Sussex Lane. Woodland. Why *here* rather than *there,* why *there* rather than *here . . .* ? He belongs nowhere, really. Might as well have been flung out of a car window at birth. Crumpled up like a used napkin and tossed away. Tears threaten, he is so oddly moved, perhaps it *does* have something to do with the *Magnus Realtors For Sale* sign and the curtainless windows and Cynthia's voice in his ear, small and chatty and impersonal, and Donald in, where was it, Connecticut or Massachusetts, and Teddy shouting from another room *I hate him, I don't want to talk to him, I HATE him!* Is it my fault that I crave life, Edwin thinks. He secures the paper cup between his knees and lights the cigar again; the nasty thing keeps going out.

Zanche. Her strong wiry arms and legs. Her deep-throated cries of anguish and triumph, which often alarm him. After-ward they lie stunned together and Edwin says in a voice trembling with gratitude, I love you, I have never loved any other woman, and Zanche lets an arm fall across his damp chest, and says with an irritated laugh: Oh bugger off, will you. *Love!*

Because (dare he think so?) she is afraid of loving him.

Because Valentin Rok has hurt her, and other men have hurt her.

Because, Edwin thinks passionately, the world fears and de-spises genuine love.

He told Bushy that, not long ago. Or was it Bagot. Or that inquisitive son of a bitch Walter Loerke in the New York office who seems to know so much about his private life. *The world fears and despises genuine love. And wants to crush it.*

Zanche and Edwin. High on hashish bought from a woman friend of Steffie's. Slow-moving, floating, detached as in a dream. Making love on the mattress on the floor. Dirty twisted sheets. Odor of paint, turpentine. Chrissie sleeping in the other room, what if she is still awake and listening, spy-ing . . . ? The thought of it makes Edwin's heart beat more

185

quickly. Disgusting of course. Unpleasant. Yet exciting too, he would be dishonest if he tried to deny it. (Fortunately Zanche has never inquired, would never think to inquire.) Am I the person who is doing these things, Edwin wonders frequently, amazed.

An added complication, that the child should be a witness. An innocent witness. The memory of Edwin and what he does with her mother will be imprinted into her consciousness, perhaps, permanently. She will always remember him. Edwin Locke. Her mother's lover. One of her mother's lovers. She will *always remember*. Because she is so young, because she is innocent, blank and featureless as the moon. She will always remember him, and isn't that as much of immortality as one can ask? With a pang of anger Edwin thinks that women like Zanche and Iris and Risa and the others are so experienced, so jaded, so *worn*, they would be incapable of remembering him for long; it is unlikely that he can matter very deeply to them. The bitches.... But little Chrissie is another case. Little Chrissie is not a woman yet. She is, oddly, not even a *girl*—not exactly. He has seen her watching him out of that blank bland maddening face and he has wondered, he has wondered, how much she knows, how much she comprehends. For instance: suppose in play he touched her, ran his hands lightly over her breasts, what then? What exactly would she *know?*

I am not the person who does these things, Edwin thinks, sucking timidly at the cigar. I am the person to whom these things are done.

The shame of that Saturday night. Hilarity too. If you care to see it from that angle. Edwin isn't certain how it came about, some of Steffie's guests were gone and others had arrived, it must have been very late, past 3 A.M., Zanche was draped over a broken-bottomed sofa with a cigarette burning between her fingers, Rok himself was beginning to feel the effects of the pills and all he'd had to drink, Edwin was a bit unsteady on his feet but enjoying himself, in these past few months he had learned for the first time in his life to *enjoy himself* frankly and honestly and candidly and without inhibition . . . and a heavily made-up girl rushed into the room, shrieking with laughter, obviously very drunk, and threw herself into Rok's arms. Who was it? Why was everyone so amused? Edwin pushed closer, tried to join the group nearest Rok and the girl. He half-envied Rok, that an attractive young woman, evidently a stranger, should appear suddenly out of nowhere and throw herself into his arms and kiss him wetly on the lips.

"Hey, who are you? What's going on here?" Edwin asked the girl, good-naturedly. His voice alarmed him, it was so reedy and nasal.

She turned to him, blinking with exaggerated solicitude.

"Why, I know you," she trilled. "I've heard all about *you.*"

Inch-long spiky eyelashes, stiff with mascara; glaring-red lipsticked lips; springy blond hair; a large quivering bosom; a very short skirt made of some tacky silver material; knee-high leather boots of the sort majorettes wear. She gave off an odor of perfume so strong that Edwin's eyes watered. So sluttish, whorish, and yet attractive, he couldn't deny that he found her attractive, though of course he didn't let on. He wouldn't give the cheeky bitch the satisfation.

"Edwin Locke, aren't you! Now don't deny it! *I know all about you!*"

And to Edwin's astonishment she flung herself at him, into his arms; she pressed her enormous breasts against his chest, fairly bounding against him, while everyone roared with laughter. Edwin tried to squirm out of her embrace and at the time time he tried to join in the laughter—he couldn't bear it that Zanche's friends might be laughing at *him.*

"Oh lover! Lover! You're the most marvelous lover of all!"

187

the girl squealed.

Edwin tried to escape, the girl clutched at him, Valentin Rok gave her a rough shove so that she stumbled against Edwin, and somehow Edwin slipped to his knees, fell heavily to the floor, while the laugher grew wilder, the ceiling spun crazily, he was terrified he would be sick to his stomach. On his hands and knees on the dirty floor he stared up, blinking the sweat out of his eyes, quite astonished to see—or was he imagining it!—the girl snatch off her blond wig, and her tight-fitting red blouse, to reveal some sort of contraption: a corset with stiff pointed cones, stuffed with foam rubber. Her—his—chest was covered with fine dark hairs. "Surprise, lover! Surprise!" Terry was shrieking, waving his blond wig like a cap.

The laughter swelled upward like a wave. Edwin waited for it to break and engulf and drown him, but somehow it did not. He simply remained there on his hands and knees, gaping, gawking, utterly astonished.

With a special garden instrument Howard Maccabee is fussing at the edge of his black-top drive, digging out crab grass. Edwin, moved suddenly by an emotion he cannot interpret, rolls down his window and calls out to him. "Howard! Hello! How are you!"

Maccabee turns. He stares at Edwin.

"Howard? It's Edwin. How are you? Lovely Sunday, isn't it?"

Maccabee looks no older than Edwin remembers. A small, trim man, with his grey hair cut a little too short, almost in an old-fashioned crew cut; not a very exciting conversationalist, but a perfectly fine neighbor. Perhaps he will invite Edwin in for a drink. It's been many months, possibly even a year, since they have seen each other.

"Howard . . . ?"

Maccabee continues to stare at him, without recognition. And then, finally, to cover his embarrassment at not knowing someone who obviously knows him (for Howard Maccabee, like most Woodland residents, is socially gracious and naturally polite), he smiles and nods and waves, silently shaping *Hello.* And then turning back to his edging instrument.

Odd. Very odd.

But perhaps Maccabee's vision has deteriorated . . . ?

Edwin, rebuffed, hurt, slightly angry, secures his paper cup between his knees and drives away. The hell with Maccabee, the hell with Cynthia, the hell with Sussex Lane. He realizes with a small thrill of satisfaction that he will never return.

Sussex Lane to curving Waldrop Pass to Mayfair Hollow to Siskin Pass to Fairway Drive to Hawthorne Drive to Mays Lane to Labyrinth Way. . . . He drives carefully, trying to remember the way out, the paper cup held firmly between his knees.

XIV.

Rok

On the morning of August 29 the charred remains of a human body are to be found in an underpass, a never-completed underpass, near the northbound Ringer Expressway. Ten or twelve steps down, past a weathered sawhorse and flapping torn sheets of polyethelene, amid old newspapers, dessicated leaves, debris soaked and baked and mellowed into a homogenous substance . . . at the very end of the cul-de-sac of East Nash Street, an area of vacant warehouses and boarded-up buildings. . . . Two black children, nine and ten years of age, are to discover the body, the thing, which will strike them at once as human, because of its size. Other children, called over to investigate, will argue that it is a dog. A very large dog. No, it's got some kind of necklaces on, those are gold necklaces, one of the children will protest, and another will reply, So's a dog sometimes, they got collars don't they?

Still, eventually, the police will be called. It's just more trouble, the mother of one of the children will say sourly. The thing could be there all year, over the winter and everything, and nobody'd know, but *you*—you guys had to go find him, didn't you!

Edwin dreams though he is not asleep. He is *not asleep*. Working late at Monarch Life & Auto Insurance, past eight

191

o'clock, the summer sky still light, a gentle bruised blue, several days' work to be crowded in, he has begun to fall behind, his hands tremble, the Scotch he keeps in his desk drawer isn't much help, his mind keeps darting and jumping about, Zanche and Chrissie, Zanche and Chrissie, Zanche lying to him, Zanche hinting that she'd like to go to Spain alone, maybe he could join her after a week or two, I need to come to terms with certain paradoxes in my art, she says evasively, I need to pursue an image to its culminating point and you would never understand. Hurt, sullen. Red-faced Edwin. I too can be angry, he whispers. I too can lose my temper at being made a fool of, exploited. Laughed about. (Do they laugh about me? No, they care for me; they are genuinely fond of me. Not just Zanche but Steffie, and Terry, and Joey, and the others. And of course Chrissie. They care for me, we've grown to know and respect one another over the months.) . . . I can be angry and unreasonable and throw things around too, don't underestimate me, Edwin whispers to Zanche's departing back.

Zanche, his love. And Chrissie, his child. Step-child. Daughter I never had. And. . . . Well. . . . And Valentin Rok also: he works in Zanche's studio during the day, when Edwin is in Wainboro, no need for them to lie no need for Zanche to swear that it's a woman friend of hers, a married woman who hasn't any studio of her own; quite apart from the stink of cigars Edwin would *know*.

And in the evenings, frequently, a telephone call. And Zanche mumbling an excuse. And hurrying out. . . . I'll be right back, Edwin, it's Steffie feeling low again, the poor thing just needs someone to talk to, all of her other friends have fled because she's so boring. Zanche running a comb through her hair, Zanche glancing surreptitiously in that old lead-backed mirror propped up against the wall. Chrissie won't be any trouble, just make her go

192

to bed if she acts up. Give her a few swats and she'll be quiet. . . .

Valentin Rok in the open doorway of D.B.'s studio. Filling the doorway with his bulk. Wild-haired, obviously high, glittering teeth and eyes and rings, saying not a word to blushing Edwin but closing one eye in an intimate wink. He knows, Edwin thinks, sickened. He knows that I know.

Money. A little problem about money.

Who is giving money to whom, who is siphoning it off and giving it to. . . . Ah yes, siphoning: it took him weeks to catch on that someone at 1616 Cray was siphoning gas out of his tank. When he told Zanche she said furiously: I know exactly who it is! I'll talk to the son of a bitch! . . . And afterward he had no trouble. With the gas.

Money. A little problem.

Edwin Locke, sipping his drink. At his enormous cluttered teakwood desk, high above the expressway and its delicate misty curls of exhaust. All is well, really: no competition: Ralph Geddes is now in Intensive Care. Edwin Locke dreaming though he is not asleep. He cannot afford to sleep, he must get his work done, he's falling behind and must get it done and will get it done before he leaves the office. . . . An immense hill into which he wants to burrow. Head-first. Trembling with desire. Sobbing with desire. And the hill becomes flesh, and the flesh seems to flinch from his violence, his need, whimpering as if it were alive; but still he forces himself into it. Like this! Like this! Like this! And as he forces himself into it it does give way, it succumbs, he pounds at it with his head, plunging, burrowing, half-choking with the rage of his desire, until he has penetrated my very core. Like this! he cries. Oh God like this!

And then the flesh, which has parted for him, in fear of him, begins to contract.

And, horribly, he is caught in me. Trapped.

193

Swallowed alive!

He screams for help, for release. But of course no one hears. His screams are not audible, nor is there anyone to hear. For I have him now, I have him fast, and tight, in the hot tight blood-thrumming depths of me, and he will never withdraw, no matter how frantically he struggles to get free, no matter how valiantly his poor strained heart beats: I have him, I have him forever.

□ □ □

You have every right to be contemptuous, he told me once, to laugh at me, it's the oldest story in the world, isn't it?—but still I want to live—*I want to live.*

Fool. Vain selfish deluded fool. His death is fast approaching but it can't be said that he has any genuine premonition of it. He simply doesn't want to get old, doesn't want to lose his "charm." I can't credit him with any insight, any depth. The final belief, it has been said (but not by one of *my* lovers), is to believe in a fiction, a metaphor, which you know to be a fiction, there being nothing else; you must love it as if it were . . . something more, and less, than a fiction. In that way you are transformed, made (for a time) immortal.

My lovers, however, are mortal.

Edwin Locke, though he never guessed it, was mortal.

There is more to me than you know, he sobs angrily. You haven't given me a chance— You haven't given me my life—

No, he hadn't the insight. He never understood.

You've misjudged me! he tells the child, who has scrambled up on her bed, her cot, standing bare-footed and stolid and damply pale in a cheap cotton nightgown that does not quite cover her bunchy knees. All of you! Your mother and—and the others— All the others— Bitches—

The child stares with a queer blank arrogance. Her round plump face is indecipherable as foam rubber.

She's downstairs with him right now, isn't she?—with her lover? As if I don't know what's going on. *As if you could deceive me.*

He steps forward, unsteady on his feet. The tiny over-warm room reels. Something underfoot—a distressing clatter—he has kicked one of the little silver finger-cymbals Chrissie has been playing with most of the day. (A gift from a friend, brought back from India, Zanche explained, brazenly fixing him with a "straightforward" stare—as if he didn't know perfectly well that the cymbals were presents from Rok. From Rok and no one else!)

Tell the truth! You can talk if you want to! You're perfectly normal when you want to be, just as your mother says!

A quarter to ten. The telephone. She and he had been waiting for it, oh yes waiting, no need to dissemble, to pretend, otherwise why her nervousness, the studied *slowness* of her walk to the phone (though of course she is nearby, there isn't any danger that Edwin will answer it), the bright calm artificial tone of her voice. Oh yes, Steffie. Oh yes. All right. No, no, I understand, no, you aren't interrupting, I'll be right down, it's fine, Edwin won't mind, of course he won't mind, anyway Chrissie's in bed. . . .

Edwin wants to stand. Wants to confront her. But his legs are weak, he doesn't trust his knees, my God how humiliating if he falls back helplessly onto the sofa, she will think he is drunk, she will be contemptuous of him as she was (oh don't deny it, don't deny it) the night before, or was it two nights before: the bout of vomiting, blood coming up too, choking and sobbing with rage as well as alarm. How can this be happening! How can this be happening to me!

195

Zanche unlike the woman he knows. Zanche flicking water on her face, running a broken comb through her hair. A veiled gaze gliding onto itself in the mirror. Bitch. Liar. Slut. And very excited, isn't she, in the pit of her belly, in the pit of her unclean groin, knowing that her lover Rok awaits and knowing what he will do to her.

Lying about him. Taking Edwin's money and giving it to *him*. And lying. I told you this woman is an old friend of mine, she just drops by in the afternoon for a few hours, she doesn't have a studio of her own, for Christ's sake her stuff doesn't *bother* you, does it? Zanche shouted. Edwin wanted to examine it, leaf through the oversized sketchbook, but Zanche forbade him. I respect her privacy and you should too, she said.

And what of that? Edwin, said, sneering, pointing at Rok's old "sculpture." (It had been pushed—Rok must have pushed it himself—into a corner of the studio.)

What do you mean? What *of* it? Zanche said.

Who moved it? Why? Who's got the right to touch that ugly thing?

I moved it, Zanche said.

Oh you did!

Yes I did! *I* did.

Afterward they smoked together, and calmed down, and Zanche said while stroking the small of his back: People have been coming and going in my life for decades, and that's just how it is. You come first, of course, but there are others too. I might seem like an isolated person to you but actually I can't live without my friends. . . .

But I come first, Edwin said softly. It was a question, not quite a statement.

Of course, don't you know that? Zanche said with a bright broad smile, the way she smiled when she was making a conscious effort to be kind, to be sweet, to be fair, to be *motherly*

196

to Chrissie.

Sometimes I don't know what I know, Edwin murmured groggily. I mean—the extent of what I know. *I just don't know.*

Poor lamb, Zanche giggled.

□ □ □

The next day, the day after. The evening of the next day. Edwin's skull hurting. Buzzing. His first mistake, to get to his feet; then his arm flailing about desperately, knocking over a vase of old dusty pussywillows Chrissie had picked that spring (so Zanche said) in a culvert nearby. The cheap vase smashed into a hundred pieces, the pussywillow branches went flying across the dirty carpet, Zanche was able to take advantage of the confusion and Chrissie's yelps of dismay to deflect attention from herself. Oh for Christ's sweet sake look what you've done! I should send you home to wherever you belong for the night—Place Rivière or whatever the fuck it is—I should send you home to your own territory to sleep it off! You're ruining my studio! You're upsetting my little girl!

So in all innocence she sneaks away. Tiptoes away. Just to visit poor Steffie, she coos, kissing him on the lips. His cold prim lips. Be back by midnight but don't wait up for me, I'll slip in beside you and wake you with a nice surprise, bet you can't guess what it is . . . !

Shivering. Trembling. Fairly sighing in his face. (What *does* Rok do to her—what do they do together? Perhaps, Edwin thinks wildly, they would allow him—someday—to be a witness. If. If, oh God, it were phrased diplomatically, gracefully. If, perhaps, he mentioned a certain respectful sum.)

You're not angry? Truly not angry?

Of course not, Edwin says.

His sickened jeering smile, which she ignores. Tiptoeing

197

away. Don't wait up for me, Edwin, she calls from the doorway with a cheerful gesture of farewell.

Oh of course not, Edwin says.

Milk-and-whiskey for Chrissie. And animal crackers, to soak in the drink, the cloying disgusting powerful drink, enought to make poor Edwin gag. A secret between us, a special treat, he whispers, no one will ever know. . . . Chrissie giggles, delighted. Eats ravenously. Busy fingers, tongue. Flesh jiggling inside the thin cotton nightie. Let me lean back here against the pillow, Edwin giggles, there's room for us both, no one will ever know. Damp crumbs dribbling down the child's front. Flakes in the corners of her mouth.

Hungry. Greedy. Insatiable child.

Tickling. High-pitched giggling.

Oh no you don't, oh no you don't, he squeals as she tries to escape.

Kicking of bedclothes, mattress. The little bed quakes.

Despite her furious elbows and threshing head the nightgown is pulled up, pulled up and off. And—

And then—

Oh my God, Edwin gasps.

He stares. Stares. Thrusts the child slowly from him and presses back against the wall, his head against the wall. Oh my God. No. It can't be. No. *No.*

Groggy, blinking. Waves of nausea: has had too much to drink, is imagining things. Nightmare. Horror. Imagination.

For Chrissie, it seems, is not a normal child. She is, it seems, not a girl—not exactly.

No, Edwin whispers.

Though her little breasts have begun to plump out, as Edwin had noticed, there is, incredibly, sadly, between her thighs, in a thin, silky patch of blond-brown hair, a small penis: pink as if it were made of rubber, and *very* small. About the size of Edwin's little finger.

198

Seeing it he begins to scream. At last, to scream, to strike out, to kick. The child is kicked off the bed, against the other wall; he hears, or thinks he hears, the thud of her head striking the baseboard.

No! No! I won't tolerate it! I won't allow it!

A blood-dimmed rage. Vision blotched with blood. The bed turned over, springs and mattress dumped, bedclothes catching against his feet, his maddened legs and thighs.

I'll kill you— All of you—

In the other room, smashing, tearing. His heart hammering in his throat. Jars overturned, stinking paintbrushes flying, a quarter-full bottle of Old Crow, the mirror splattered with paint, dirty plates cascading to the floor, the sketchbook torn, its pages madly torn, a tumbler encrusted with filth thrown against the window—smashing the window— The mirror overturned, crashing to the floor; the hard-backed chair, the table with Zanche's supplies on it, the portable television set—

Bastards! Murderers! I'll kill you all—

A scissors in hand, slashing at Rok's sculpture. The lightweight Styrofoam is easily ripped, lengths of twine and string become entangled with his wrist, he shouts at the thing as he murders it, half-choking with laughter. O this is easy! This is miraculously easy! Why didn't I do this long ago!

Gasoline? Turpentine? Maybe he can burn the place down—

But: suddenly they are in the room with him. The others. They are shouting for him to stop. Valentin Rok, and Zanche, and Steffie, and D.B., and Joey, and someone he has never seen before, an oily-skinned black man in a handwoven vest, and someone else, shouting for him to stop. Grabbing at his arms. Trying to wrest the scissors from him.

Rok, it is. Struggling with him.

He strikes out, catching Rok on the side of the head. And brings his arm back in a wide furious swing, raking the tip of

199

the scissors—the very tip!—across the man's cheek.

The surprise of Rok's blood, leaping out. As if alive. As if eager to fly into the air.

Then they are wrestling together on the floor, on the bunched-up carpet. Zanche is screaming. Zanche is kicking at him. Shards of mirror, broken glass, tubes of paint, brushes, trowels, the odor of whiskey, the startling sight of blood: and Valentin Rok straddling him, his huge hands tightening around Edwin's throat.

Somehow Edwin breaks free. Scrambles on his hands and knees. It is the black man who has pulled Rok away, and now fat perspiring D.B. tries to grab hold of Edwin, to stop him. No you don't! No you don't! Edwin screams. He gets to his feet, stooped, running, somehow he is running, staggering, colliding blindly with the doorframe, pushing someone away. Then he is in the corridor. On the stairs. Above him Zanche's voice rises.

Chrissie— He did something to Chrissie—

Stumbling downstairs, half-naked, one shoe off, panting, gasping, sobbing. They are not going to catch him. They are not going to catch *him*. His car, parked close to the warehouse entrance: but his car keys, where are— Rok is too near, Rok is only a few yards behind. So Edwin flees shirtless into the warm August night, running with one shoe on and one shoe off, down East Nash Street, his breath shuddering in his throat.

Elsewhere in the city there are sirens, faint, ghostly, almost musical. Distant. Police sirens, or fire sirens, who can tell?— they are too distant. Miles away, on the west side, smokestacks rise into the clouds, which they illuminate, rosily. At the city airport two restless searchlights cross and recross each other's path. In the heart of the North American metropolis! Edwin, gasping for air, seems to have outrun his pursuers suddenly. He has turned a corner, or darted into an alley, no he has discovered a secret tunnel, he plunges forward and catches sight of me waiting for him . . . and sobbing with gratitude he is about to throw himself into my embrace when Rok seizes him cruelly by the hair.

No you don't! Oh no you don't, *you!*

Edwin shrieks with pain.

Zanche is striking at him. And someone else, fairly spitting with rage, tries to get at him, crying, Kill him! Don't let him escape again!

Child-molester!

Rapist!

Fascist swine!

Panting waddling wild-eyed Steffie. *But didn't she care for him!*

Don't let him escape, he'll go to the police, he'll get us all arrested—

Don't worry, the bastard isn't going to escape!

A stabbing sensation in his shoulder, in his chest. Rok is bringing the scissors down again. Again. O my God don't, O I beg of you don't, don't, the pain is—

But there is no blood, why is there no blood? His flesh hasn't even been penetrated. Wait, he whispers, this is real, O God this is *real*, it hurts, my heart, my heart, I think it's my heart, please don't do it, I beg of you, I beg—

Impatient exasperated Valentin Rok strikes him on the back of the neck and he stumbles forward. There is no blood, there is no scissors, the pain is stabbing but intermittent . . . if he can only crawl over the chain-link fence and up the incline to the expressway . . . if he can only flag down a car . . . ask to be taken to the hospital, to the emergency ward . . . if he can get up there on the expressway someone will stop for him, someone will save him, *must* save him. . . .

Contemptible fascist exploiter!

Molester of children!

201

Pig!

Rok seizes him again by the hair. And forces him backward, so that his spine threatens to crack. O God the pain. Bleeding from many wounds. Innumerable wounds. Rok's whiskey-rich breath in his face, Rok's bulging maddened eyes. Why such rage, such hatred? What have I done? Why—

In mid-air, it seems, he dies: Edwin Locke dies: and collapses into Rok's arms, bringing Rok with him to the pavement.

Dies.

And falls: is dead, in fact, before he strikes the pavement.

But the others are not placated. It's a trick, one of the fucker's tricks! Don't let him escape!

Finish him off!

Kick him in the—

He might have a knife, watch out—

Here's a knife!

Rok gets to his feet. Though his face and shirt are smeared with blood he manages to move with a certain self-conscious dignity.

Get me some gasoline, he says.

Is he—?

Some gasoline. You. And hurry.

Oh my God, is he dead?

He's—?

Rok, in a classic gesture, prods the body with his foot; turns it over slowly with his foot. Limp, and heavy. Very heavy.

Valentin, is he—?

The son of a bitch! Isn't this just like him!

Zanche begins to scream. She crouches over the body, striking at it with her fists, until one of them pulls her away.

Just like him! O the selfish swinish bastard! Raping my little girl and tearing the studio apart and destroying my life and now—now—

Rok and D.B. drag the body by its ankles some yards away, to the underpass. Both men move quickly, grunting.

Nobody ever comes here, not even kids. Nobody will ever find him.

—identification?—car keys—

Up on the expressway, not more than a hundred yards away, traffic is passing as usual, as always: a steady thrumming vibrating drone.

Peace.

Secrecy.

Nobody will ever find him. The bastard.

Odd: in the heart of our great imperial cities, in certain deserted or forgotten areas, it is very nearly silent.

. . . that gasoline?

Last autumn's leaves, dessicated sheets of newspaper, nameless debris. Hardy clumps of Queen Anne's lace, buttercups, and heal-alls, growing, as if by miracle, in a few inches of fortuitous soil. But Rok and D.B. take no notice.

Heavy twat, isn't he.

Edwin's crumpled body, rolling to the bottom of the steps. A smear of blood—not his own—across his forehead and nose, and gleaming strangely in the pale light of a nearby streetlamp; his eyes all white, rolled to the back of his head; his sporty peach-colored shirt hanging in filmy shreds at his waist. Get the son of a bitch's wallet, Rok says, his teeth chattering with excitement. The shoe too. Hurry.

Someone hands him the container of gasoline. He unscrews the cap, and dribbles gas over the body. Takes his time. The others back away, they are leading Zanche away, peace has been restored, peace of a sort has been restored, the sirens are many miles away, the searchlights harass each other on the far side of the city. Rok forces himself to act with caution, even with a certain ceremonial grace, despite the undeniable tension of the moment.

203

Oh hurry, Zanche's voice calls, faintly, feebly.

The container is empty. Rok rubs his hard calloused fingers over the handle several times, to smudge his fingerprints. The night is very still. There are crickets, improbably. No need to act in haste, no need to panic, it will be accomplished, it will be consummated, and with a certain style. After all he is Valentin Rok.

Evil exploitative fascist swine, Rok whispers.

He is having difficulty with the cigarette lighter. The damn thing never works at first. You have to keep trying, and not get impatient: one two three four *five*.

Printed October 1979 in Santa Barbara & Ann Arbor for
the Black Sparrow Press by Mackintosh and Young &
Edwards Brothers Inc. Design by Barbara Martin. This
edition is published in paper wrappers; there are 1000 cloth
trade copies; 300 hardcover copies have been numbered &
signed by the author; & 50 deluxe copies have been
handbound in boards by Earle Gray & are numbered &
signed by the author.

Photo: Graeme Gibson

Joyce Carol Oates has been called "the best young novelist
in the United States today." *Cybele* is the ninth book by Ms.
Oates to be published by Black Sparrow Press, the others
being *The Hostile Sun: The Poetry of D.H. Lawrence* (1973),
The Hungry Ghosts (1974), *Miracle Play* (1974), *The
Seduction & Other Stories* (1975), *The Triumph of the
Spider Monkey* (1976), *Daisy* (1977), *Season of Peril* (1977),
and *All the Good People I've Left Behind* (1979).

Joyce Carol Oates is married to Raymond Smith, and both
are Professors of English at the University of Windsor,
Ontario, where they teach and edit the literary magazine
Ontario Review. They are presently living in Princeton,
New Jersey, where Ms. Oates is Visiting Writer at Princeton
University for the academic year 1979-1980. She is currently
working on a long novel called *Bellefleur*.